$4 —

2 $\frac{40}{XX}$

May 9, 1996
Houston Tx
BX Warehouse

D1256707

Splinter's Pard

SPLINTER'S PARD

Gene Tuttle

AVALON BOOKS
THOMAS BOUREGY AND COMPANY, INC.
401 LAFAYETTE STREET
NEW YORK, NEW YORK 10002

© Copyright 1987 by Gene Tuttle
Library of Congress Catalog Card Number: 87-91644
ISBN 0-8034-8657-X

PRINTED IN THE UNITED STATES OF AMERICA
BY HADDON CRAFTSMEN, SCRANTON, PENNSYLVANIA

Splinter's Pard

CHAPTER ONE

THE morning sun was rising from the hills to the east, and it flung long shadows across the mesquite-covered terrain. There was still a coolness in the air as Splinter McGee rode slowly beside the railroad tracks. He was letting his horse, Ranger, take his time. He was in no hurry to reach Santa Nella.

Splinter had left El Cajon before dawn, hoping to make the twenty-mile ride in time for breakfast. This was his first time in Santa Nella County.

"Funny," he said, running his long, lean fingers through Ranger's mane. "This coun-

1

try doesn't look any different from what we've been ridin' through."

Ahead was a small bridge over a riverbed without a drop of water. The bridge was about twenty feet across, but Splinter knew that Ranger would prefer to go down the slight bank and cross the dry wash before resuming the ride along the tracks.

As they swung across the dry wash, something under the bridge caught Splinter's eye, and he drew up his reins. Leaning forward on his saddle horn, he peered under the bridge.

Someone was huddled in a blanket. The person had his back to Splinter and the blanket was pulled up over his head. The tall, lean cowboy studied the figure for a moment, then he swung down out of his saddle and dropped his reins.

"Howdy," he said, approaching the traveler who might be in need of a helping hand.

Suddenly the blanket few open, and a young boy appeared. He rolled over to face Splinter, a six-shooter gripped tightly in his two small hands.

"Don't come any closer!" he warned. "My trigger finger's just itchin'."

Splinter eyed the young man, who was

about ten years old. "Whatever you say, pardner. It's kind of early for an argument."

"Tryin' to sneak up on me, weren't you? That's the only way they'll ever take me to that orphanage."

"Orphanage?" Splinter rubbed the side of his nose. "I don't know what you're talking about, pardner. I'm a stranger here."

The boy's eyes studied Splinter, but the gun never wavered an inch.

"How do I know you ain't from the orphanage?"

"I wouldn't know the local orphanage from the local brewery. I was just ridin' through on my way to Santa Nella."

"Then get goin'," the boy snapped.

Splinter rubbed his chin thoughtfully while his steel-gray eyes studied the boy. "Where are you going, pardner?" he drawled.

The boy thought for a second, then replied, "I'm not sure yet, but it'll be a long way from here." He swallowed hard and sniffed, but the gun barrel held still.

Splinter showed his friendliness with a smile. He understood youngsters, and this boy was in trouble and in need of a friend.

"Pardner," he said softly, "if you'll put

down that six-shooter, maybe we can talk a little."

"There's nothin' to talk about," the boy said. "My mind's made up!"

Splinter nodded. "I've felt that way many times, but a little talk can make things look brighter. I ain't going to make you do anything you don't want to."

The boy considered what Splinter had said. He sniffed again as he slowly lowered the six-shooter.

"I'll talk, but keep your distance," he said.

Splinter dropped to his haunches. "Tell me why you're supposed to go to an orphanage."

The boy tried to blink away the tears in his blue eyes. He shook his head, let go of the gun with his left hand, and rubbed his eyes.

"That bad, huh?" Splinter said.

The boy nodded. "Some people in Santa Nella want to put me in an orphanage."

"Why?"

"They think I can't live by myself."

"Where are your parents?"

"Mom died six years ago," he replied softly, then he looked down at the six-shooter as he added, "Dad was killed two days ago."

"I'm mighty sorry to hear that," Splinter said.

"You are?"

Splinter nodded. "Lost my parents when I was about your age. Indians killed 'em, and I've been on my own ever since."

The boy looked with admiration at Splinter. "You look like you've done right well on your own."

"That's because I had a little help from a friend who gave me good advice."

"That's what I need too. But I ain't got no friends in Santa Nella."

"No friends at all?" Splinter asked.

"Well, there's Miss Skelly, my teacher. And also the sheriff. But they wouldn't be too much help to me now."

"Do you live in Santa Nella?"

The boy shook his head. "Dad and I had a little ranch outside of town about three miles. I wanted to stay, but some folks think I should be put in an orphanage. I ran away last night."

"Would you care to hear some advice?"

"Go ahead," the boy said. "You sound like Dad."

"Why don't you take charge of the ranch, and for a spell I could be your foreman. That way, there'd be someone at the ranch helping you—but you'd be the boss."

The boy thought it over for a while, then shook his head.

"How could I pay you? I don't have any money," he said.

"Money ain't everything. I'm sure we could work that out in time."

The boy's face broke into a grin. "I think I'm goin' to like that,—I didn't catch your name."

"I never throwed it, pardner." Splinter laughed as he stepped forward, his right hand extended. "My handle's Splinter McGee."

"I'm Jim Lane, but everyone calls me Peanuts."

"I take it you like peanuts," Splinter said with a grin.

"Sure do," the boy said as he shoved the big six-shooter inside his belt. "Do you like 'em?"

"Never yet turned down a goober. Let me help you with your gear."

In a few minutes the boy's few possessions were wrapped into the blanket and fastened with a rope.

"Ranger likes to ride double," Splinter said as he fastened the roll to the back of the saddle. Then he helped the boy up behind the saddle too.

Peanuts pointed the way to the Lazy L ranch. "It ain't much to look at, but Dad built it," he told Splinter as they rode along.

"Bet it's a castle," Splinter said, laughing.

Splinter McGee was six feet four and weighed one hundred eighty, and he was as hard as nails, as some men had learned. He was fast with six-guns and fists. His lean face was deeply tanned from the sun, and between his steel-gray eyes was a long, hooked nose that had a habit of poking into other folks' business. Beneath his nose was a wide mouth that looked like a mere slit until he smiled.

His clothes were typical western, dusty, and with much wear and tear. His gun belt sagged in just the right places, and his holster was always in position for a quick draw of his Colt .45. His boots were worn, and his sombrero, though battered, protected his eyes from the sun and kept the heat from his sandy-colored hair.

Peanuts Lane was ten years old, fairly tall for his age, but very thin. He wore overalls held up by a rope belt and a gray shirt that showed many washings. He wore boots but no hat on his head, exposing his thatch of red hair.

Splinter turned and looked down at the

boy. "Do you feel like talking—especially about your Dad?" he asked.

"I guess I can, Mr. McGee."

"My name's Splinter—McGee was my pa."

"It—it happened a couple of nights ago. We had finished dinner and was sittin' at the table when we heard someone ride into the yard. The dogs barked a lot. We wondered who it was, then a man called Dad. Dad went to the door and when he opened it someone shot him. I ran to the window and saw a man ridin' away in a hurry. I looked at Dad, but he was still, so I got my horse and rode to get the doctor and the sheriff. When we got home, Doc Forbes said Dad was dead—shot with buckshot!"

"Did you see the killer?"

"Yeah—but it was just gettin' dark and it was hard to see much because he was ridin' away fast," Peanuts replied. "The sheriff asked me the same thing."

"Who hated your Dad enough to kill him?"

"Ever since we came here, King Ward's been tryin' to get our ranch 'cause of the good spring we have. He owns most of the valley, but he don't own our place. Then there's a Mr. Harris who wanted to buy the ranch, but Dad turned him down. He got real mad and threatened Dad. And I reckon there's more that would like to see Dad dead."

"Who's this Harris fellow?"

"He came here a few months ago. Some say he was here a long time ago. I only saw him a couple of times, but he sure can get mad."

"Sounds like an interesting place," Splinter said. "It sure was tough about your dad."

"But you know somethin', Splinter? I never cried. Miss Skelly said maybe I ought to. She said it would help me inside."

"I reckon she's right," Splinter said. "When my folks were killed by Indians, I cried for a week or more."

"You did, huh?"

"And I wasn't ashamed of it, Peanuts. It made me feel a lot better."

Peanuts nodded thoughtfully and pointed to their right. "Our ranch is just around that bend there, Splinter."

They rode on in silence until they rounded the point in the hills. Splinter drew up on the reins and Ranger stopped.

"That's it," Peanuts said proudly. "Dad built it—and he always said that I helped him. But I was too small then to do much. Dad and me came here from Ohio after Mom died. He bought the ranch from a funny old man. There wasn't a house, just a couple of sheds. We lived in them for a year until we got the house built."

"It looks great," Splinter said. He nudged Ranger and they started down a winding cattle trail toward the ranch house, which was situated amid a grove of sycamores. Behind the house were a small stable and a corral, partly hidden by the huge trees. They were riding in from the rear, and Ranger swung across the yard and around the corner of the house to the front.

Suddenly Splinter drew up quickly on the reins, his eyes mere slits, his right hand dropping to his holster. A couple of horses were tied to a hitching post in front, and two men were sitting on the edge of the porch, watching them.

Peanuts told Splinter, "That's the sheriff and his deputy. Wonder what they're doin' out here?"

"We'll find out in a second, pardner," Splinter said.

Sheriff Irish Mulligan and Deputy Joe Walters watched them as they approached. The sheriff was a heavy-set man with a round, red face, small eyes, flat nose, and a wide mouth. Deputy Walters was tall and thin, with a lean face and the straggliest mustache that Splinter had ever seen. He tugged at it as he squinted at Splinter.

"Wondered where you was, Peanuts," the sheriff said. He eyed Splinter as he and the boy walked up on the porch.

"Oh, just been out, sheriff," Peanuts replied. "Want you to meet my pardner, Splinter McGee. Pard, this is Sheriff Mulligan and his deputy, Joe Walters."

The two officers shook hands with Splinter.

"Pardner, eh?" Joe grunted.

"Yeah. I reckon Peanuts needs a little help right now." Ain't no law agin it, is there?"

Mulligan shook his head. "I reckon not, but it's kind of sudden, ain't it?"

Peanuts grinned. "All of a couple of hours. Splinter's goin' to help me run the ranch. He'll be my foreman."

The two officers grinned.

"I heard that there was a movement to ship Peanuts out, but he isn't ready to leave his ranch," Splinter explained.

The sheriff said, "There's been some talk about it, but with you being here with him— Well, I reckon that'll make a difference. Did you know Peanuts before you came here?"

Splinter shook his head. "Nope, but we got a lot in common." He turned to the boy. "Want to take Ranger down to the stable and feed him for me?"

"Sure." Eagerly, Peanuts picked up the reins and led the horse toward the stable.

"This may be irregular as all get-out," Splinter said after the boy was out of sight, "but I felt sorry for him. He was running away, and we just happened to meet."

"You don't happen to be Wilbur T. McGee, do you?" the sheriff asked.

Splinter's eyes narrowed. "If you use that name again, expect fireworks. I hate it!" he snapped.

"I read about you in the bulletin we get from the Cattlemen's Association. Are you here on official business?"

"Nope," Splinter replied, shaking his head. "Just ridin' through. Might stay for a spell now, though—dependin' on the people around Santa Nella."

"Did Peanuts say anything about his father leaving a will?" the deputy asked.

"Never mentioned it. Do you suppose he left one?"

"Hank Lane was a smart man," Mulligan said. "He knew he was buckin' some tough characters around here. I suppose he left a will, but no one's thought of looking for it until now."

"It was all my idea," Joe Walters added. "It just dawned on me."

Mulligan nodded. "Perhaps Ira Crabb, our esteemed attorney-at-law, might have it. He was a friend of Hank."

"I doubt if Ira has a friend," Joe said.

"We'll check on Crabb when we get back to town."

"I'll check on him," Joe corrected. "I always get the dirty work."

"Well, for now Peanuts is taken care of," Mulligan said. "I'll let certain parties in Santa Nella know about it, McGee. Thanks a lot."

The boy returned from the stable as the two officers rode away. He waved to them and joined Splinter on the porch.

"Our things are in the stable," Peanuts said. "I didn't bring 'em up to the house."

"Fine. We'll get 'em."

"Hey, you ain't seen the inside yet." Peanuts opened the front door. "C'mon in."

The ranch house consisted of one very large room. To the left of the front door was the kitchen area with a large wood stove, a counter with open shelves, a wash basin, and a table with two chairs. Straight ahead was the living area with an old sofa, several chairs, and a table with an oil lamp on it. To the right was a double bunk built against the wall. A space closed off by a blanket on a wire was the closet. Everything was neat and clean.

"This is a castle," Splinter said.

"I reckon it'll do for now." Peanuts grinned. "I bet those two officers were surprised."

"I reckon they were. They'll see that everyone in Santa Nella knows about our partnership before sundown."

Peanuts nodded. "I hope those old women will change their minds."

"I'm sure they will." Splinter walked over to the kitchen and looked at the filled shelves. "Are you hungry?"

"I could eat a bear." Peanuts added, "That's what Dad used to say."

"Have any chickens around here?"

"I'll find some eggs." Peanuts laughed as he turned and hurried out of the house.

Splinter walked around the large room, studying everything. Near the bunks was a shelf with several books, indicating that Hank Lane had been a reader. He shoved the hanging blanket aside and saw several shirts and overalls hanging on the nails. Two sets of boots were neatly placed on the floor against the wall. Across the room, on a table behind the sofa, there were two letters, both opened. He picked them up and looked at them. They were from Ohio and addressed to Henry Lane. He put them down and moved back into the kitchen as Peanuts returned with the eggs.

"How do you like them?" Splinter asked while he started a fire in the wood stove.

"Over and smashed," Peanuts said. "Is that enough eggs?"

"That's plenty—unless you've got two hollow legs."

Splinter whipped up their breakfast while Peanuts set the table. The boy picked up the two letters and brought them back to the table when they were ready to eat.

"These came after Dad died," he said. "I couldn't read them."

"After breakfast," Splinter said.

When they had eaten their fill Splinter read the letters and then informed Peanuts:

"One is from your aunt. She asks if you are all right and how things are going. She says a Mr. Chaney has taken over the store."

"Oh, that's the store Dad started," Peanuts said. "Dad used to own a big store back in Cleveland, but after Mom died he sold out. I don't know much about the deal, but Dad still gets money from the sale. That must be from Aunt Ida—Dad's sister."

"Now for the other letter. It's from a Fred Bennett in Cleveland. Just writing to let your dad know that his mother—your grandmother—died and left everything to Ida and Henry Lane. He wants an answer on what to do with your share."

"Gee, that's too bad about Grandma," Peanuts said softly. "I don't remember her."

"I reckon I'll have to write 'em both and tell 'em what has happened here."

CHAPTER TWO

LATE afternoon, when Peanuts decided that he should catch up on his schooling, Splinter McGee rode in with him for his first view of the little cattle town that had been his destination that morning.

Santa Nella was not typical western, because the people living there took great pride in their town. Its main street was crooked because the residents did not want to cut down any of the large trees that lined both sides of it. The stores were well kept, and well painted, and all signs were readable. At the farther end was the depot and railroad, but

17

even that small yellow building was partly shaded by large trees.

"Never saw a town this pretty," Splinter said to Peanuts.

As they rode past the sheriff's office and Irish Mulligan called out to them, Peanuts excused himself, saying he had to go to school. Splinter hitched up Ranger and crossed the wooden walk to the sheriff's office.

"Talked with Ira Crabb, but he informed me that Hank Lane never made a will."

Splinter shoved his battered hat back on his head and squinted at the sheriff. "Can you trust him?" he asked.

"Ira Crabb isn't the salt of the earth, but I don't think he'd do anything irregular."

"Why is the Lazy L so valuable?"

Mulligan squinted at Splinter, thinking. "What makes you think it's valuable?"

"Why would people want to buy it—maybe go so far as to murder for it?"

"Do you think that's why Lane was shot?"

Splinter nodded. "I feel it is after talking with Peanuts. He told me that fellows named King Ward and Harris wanted the ranch badly."

Mulligan scratched the back of his neck.

"Maybe it's the water on the ranch. Lane said he had a large bubbling spring—and water is important in these parts."

"Maybe for Ward and his herds, but what about Harris? Does he own a ranch too?"

"Harris came back here about a month ago. He used to live here, but the urge for money made him slip, and he spent five years in the state pen for robbing the bank."

"Five years, eh?" Splinter's eyes narrowed. "How could he get money to buy a ranch?"

Mulligan shrugged his shoulders. Before he could speak, a small, wiry old cattleman walked into the office, stopping just inside the doorway. He glanced from the sheriff to Splinter. His face was drawn, with skin like parchment. His eyes were small and shifty, and his mouth was a slit under a stubby nose.

"What in blazes do you think you're pullin'?" he snapped, turning to face Splinter.

Splinter smiled. "I'll bet you're King Ward."

The old man flinched slightly. "How'd you know?"

"From a description. There couldn't be more than one of you. The Good Lord doesn't make mistakes often."

"Mistake, eh?" King Ward growled. "I'll tell you somethin', high pockets. You're not goin' to take over the Lane ranch."

"You've heard wrong," Splinter said. "I'm merely foreman. Peanuts Lane is the owner."

"That little kid, eh?" Ward turned to the open doorway and spat on the walk. "He can't run that ranch."

"He'll probably do a lot better job than you can," Splinter said. "He's got brains."

Ward's tight skin tightened more, and his fists were tightly clenched as he looked up at Splinter. He swayed slightly on his feet, undecided upon what to do. King Ward wasn't used to being talked to like this.

After a moment of indecision Ward whirled on his high heels and stomped out of the office. Splinter stared after him, but a chuckle caused him to turn and see the sheriff leaning forward in his chair, his eyes filling with tears as he beat his hands on the top of the desk.

"That was great!" he said. "No one ever told King Ward anything like that."

"He must think he's really a king."

Mulligan sighed. "But don't think you've got him. He's mean."

"I'll be ready for him."

"Hey, Splinter!" a voice called from outside the doorway.

Standing on the walk with Peanuts was a very attractive young woman. Splinter eyed her closely as he moved into the doorway. She was a blonde, her blue eyes shining as she looked up at him. He removed his hat and smiled at her.

"Pard, this is my teacher, Miss Skelly. Miss Skelly, this is my pardner, Splinter McGee."

"Please to meet you, miss. Peanuts has been doing some high talkin' today about you."

"He's told me all about you too." Tina Skelly smiled. "I'm sure you will be able to help him and keep him here. He's a good student."

"He's a fine young man," Splinter said as he turned to Peanuts. "Have you got your books all set?"

"Sure have. Got a lot of homework to do, but I'll catch up."

Tina Skelly said good-bye and hurried up the crooked walk as it wound around the trees. Splinter leaned against the doorway and watched her. His train of thought was broken when Peanuts tugged at his sleeve and said:

"She's sure purty, ain't she?"

"Yes, she certainly is," Splinter agreed.

"Let's go to the store. I have a feelin' I need some peanuts."

Splinter waved a hand to the sheriff, then followed Peanuts across the street and to the general store. Peanuts hurried ahead and into the store, but Splinter took his time, admiring the newly painted front, an unusual sight in a cowtown.

Sauntering into the store, he saw Peanuts talking with the clerk.

"Would you like something too?" the clerk asked.

"I don't think so," Splinter replied.

"Your credit is good here. We bill you once a month."

"I'm glad to hear that," Splinter said with a wide grin. "This is something a little different for me."

The clerk nodded and moved down the counter to help Peanuts fill his order. Splinter leaned against the counter and looked around. A cowboy came into the store and started toward the counter, but he stopped when he saw Splinter.

"Well, well, Tad Wilson, as I live and breathe," Splinter said to the cowboy.

"What are you doing here?" Wilson asked.

"Funny, I was going to ask you the same question, Tad."

"I'm going straight now," Wilson said as he moved in closer to Splinter. "I done three years—and learned my lesson."

"I'm sure glad to hear that, Tad. Where are you working?"

"I'm at the Box W. Been there about a year now. Will you be here long?"

Splinter shrugged his shoulders, then nodded toward Peanuts. "I'm staying at the Lazy L, kind of watching over my new boss."

Wilson looked at Peanuts, then back to Splinter, shaking his head.

"The Lazy L ain't a healthy place to stay," he said softly.

"I aim to make it healthy," Splinter said.

Wilson turned and walked out of the store without making his purchase. Splinter wondered why. Back in Wyoming, he had helped in convicting Wilson of rustling.

"Look at this!" Peanuts said to Splinter. He was holding a big bag of peanuts in both hands.

"That ought to take care of you for a spell."

Peanuts shook his head. "With me and you both eatin' em, they'll go fast." He paused and looked toward the doorway. "Did you know Tad Wilson?"

Splinter nodded. "A few years ago, in Wyoming. Do you know him?"

"He and Bat Rogg, the Box W foreman, rode out a few times and talked with Dad about sellin' the ranch. I don't like him."

Leaving the store, they nearly bumped into Ira Crabb.

"Howdy, Mr. Crabb," Peanuts said as he held out the bag of peanuts. "Have a peanut?"

"Thank you, Peanuts," the attorney said. Then he turned his attention to Splinter. "I presume you are Mr. McGee?"

"That's right," Splinter said.

Ira Crabb was in his fifties, of medium size but on the plump side. He wore a swallow-tailed coat, black and white checkered trousers, and a white shirt with a bright red bow tie. On his feet were patent-leather shoes, badly in need of cleaning. His round face with a bulbous nose glistened from constant scrubbing. His brown eyes peered at Splinter through glasses fastened on his nose, with a ribbon from the right rim that was fastened to his lapel.

"I saw you speaking with the sheriff," he said. "I presume he told you that Henry Lane did not leave a will and that the judge will have to decide what to do regarding Peanuts."

Splinter nodded. "But don't you think it strange that Lane wouldn't leave a will? He seemed, from what I heard, to be a good business man, and leaving a will would be good business."

"I fully agree with you. Perhaps it is hidden at the ranch. He never once mentioned a will to me, and we were very good friends— weren't we, Peanuts?"

The boy nodded as he munched on some peanuts.

"They told me his credit is good at the store," Splinter said.

"I presume it is," Crabb said. "Henry Lane always had enough money to purchase anything he desired."

"Maybe I better check at the bank."

"I think it would be best to talk with the judge first. I'm sure he will straighten matters out. Besides, no one here knows you, so I wouldn't be too hasty to get my fingers on the money."

"You've got me wrong, Crabb," Splinter

said, his eyes narrowing. "I'm here now to look out for Peanuts, and that's all! I want you to remember that."

Crabb nodded. "I'm sure you want to do what is right. Well, good day, gentlemen."

Crabb stepped past them and entered the store. Peanuts looked up at Splinter.

"I've decided not to like him any longer," he said.

"He's only doing what he thinks is right."

As they strolled up the walk they came to the Glory Be Saloon and Gambling House. Its swinging doors banged open and a burly young cowboy staggered forward into their path.

"Hey!" Peanuts yelled as his bag of nuts went flying. He staggered but kept his feet.

Splinter grabbed the cowboy and swung him around on his high heels. In a flash, Splinter realized that this man was not drunk. It had been deliberate.

"Get your filthy hands off me! What'cha lookin' at?" the cowboy growled.

"At a fool," Splinter replied. "You're not drunk!"

The man leapt forward, both fists going for Splinter, but Splinter was not there. He had sensed what was going to happen, and as the big man made his move, Splinter stepped quickly aside, letting the big man throw blows into the air.

The man whirled, bellowing like a bull, but before he could decide his next move, Splinter nailed him with a right cross to the chin, and then a left to his nose. The man staggered back and almost fell off the walk. As his nose began to bleed, he raised his right hand and rubbed it, and then looked down at the blood on his hand.

"Blast you!" he snorted as he charged again. Splinter side-stepped the charge, and caught him in the stomach with a hard right. The blow took all the wind and fight out of the big man. He staggered several steps, gasping for breath, then he fell to his knees and rolled off the walk into the street.

While Peanuts picked up his goobers, Splinter turned and looked at the saloon door, expecting someone to come to the fallen man's aid. But no one appeared.

'Let's git," Splinter said.

They retrieved their horses and rode swiftly out of town.

"Who was that gent?" Splinter asked.

"That was Bat Rogg. He musta been drunk."

"He wasn't drunk. He wanted to fight."

"He's been here a long time, and I never heard of anyone beatin' him up before. I'd watch out for him. He works for King Ward."

"And so does Tad Wilson," Splinter said.

After their supper and cleanup, Peanuts started his school homework while Splinter looked around the house. He paused at the two large books on the table next to the bunk and studied them. Both books were tightly tied with white thread that matched the covers.

Splinter rubbed his chin thoughtfully. Why would these two books be tied like that? He sat down on the bunk and picked up one of the books.

"Did your Dad ever read these books?" he asked Peanuts.

"He used to read 'em, but he hadn't for a long spell. He told me never to touch 'em."

Splinter nodded as he fingered the thread. It was tightly wound around the entire book many times and then tied in several knots.

"Do you know why he tied them up?" he asked.

"Nope."

Splinter took a knife from his pocket and cut the thread. Carefully he opened the book, and was surprised by what he saw.

"Peanuts," he said, "come over here."

Joining Splinter on the bunk, Peanuts looked down at the book, his eyes growing wide.

"Gee! Gosh!" he cried. "Where did that money come from?"

The book had been hollowed out, and in place of the pages was neatly wrapped currency.

"Your dad must have used this instead of the bank."

"But he always went to the bank for money."

"He did, huh?" Splinter picked up the other book and quickly cut the threads. It, too, was filled with currency.

"Wow!" Peanuts said. "That's all the money in the world. What are we goin' to do with it?"

"It's all yours, as far as I can see."

"It'll sure buy a lot of peanuts. But it's half yours, pard."

Splinter shook his head. "Nope—it's all yours, Peanuts. But I think we'll keep this a secret between just the two of us."

"I like secrets." The boy grinned.

While Peanuts resumed his homework,

Splinter, using a pencil and piece of paper, counted the currency. Finished, he sat back and whistled. Peanuts looked at him.

"Find more?" he asked.

Splinter shook his head. "We got to find a new place to hide this money."

"I have a good hidin' place," Peanuts said. "It's out in the stable.

Splinter rose to his feet and looked at the pile of currency stacked on the lower bunk. It was getting dark, so he lit the oil lamps on the two tables.

Splinter threw a blanket over the money, then followed the boy out of the house and down to the stable. They lit the lantern hanging inside and then Peanuts led the way into a small tack room to the right of the doorway. He shoved several saddles aside, knelt down, and pulled up a board from the floor.

"This is it," he said. "I used—"

His voice broke off, and Splinter whirled around just as a gun butt came slashing down. His move had protected his head, but the butt struck him on the left shoulder, driving him backward against the wall.

Standing inside the tack room was a masked man. He quickly reversed his six-shooter and covered Splinter and Peanuts.

"Thanks, kid," he said. "Been hopin' to find this place for a long time."

"Who are you?" Peanuts asked, still on his hands and knees, looking up at the masked man.

The man snickered as he moved toward the opening in the floor.

Leaning against the wall, his shoulder aching from the blow, Splinter watched the masked man. He wished he had his gun, but it was in the house.

As the masked man bent forward to peer into the opening, Peanuts grabbed his knees. The man tried to run away, but Splinter threw himself at him and they both fell down over Peanuts, who went sprawling across the room. The masked man's gun slithered across the floor near where Peanuts landed against the wall. The boy quickly fell on the gun and grasped it with both hands. He rolled over and sat up. But he couldn't pull the trigger because he might hit Splinter.

The masked man and Splinter wrestled across the small tack room and through the doorway into the stable. Peanuts jumped to his feet and hurried to the door, still grasping the six-shooter in both hands.

The masked man realized what he was up

against, and as he freed his right hand he slashed it down on Splinter's injured shoulder. The pain was like a burning torch, and as Splinter released his hold, the masked man jerked free, whirled around, and raced out the door.

Peanuts swung the gun and pulled the trigger. The recoil knocked him against the door, but he managed a second shot. The masked man vanished into the night.

"Nice work," Splinter grunted, as he staggered to his feet, holding his left arm. He grimaced with pain.

"Are you all right?"

"Yeah—I reckon I am."

"Sorry I missed him."

"You sure scared the devil out of him." Splinter blew out the lantern and they started toward the house.

"We'll have to find a new hidin' place," Peanuts said.

Just then a horsemen swung into the yard. It was too dark to see who it was, and Splinter quickly grabbed the gun from Peanuts.

"Howdy," a voice called.

"It's the sheriff," Peanuts said.

Irish Mulligan rode up to them by the front door.

"Who was that pulling out of here so fast?" he asked as he swung out of the saddle. "He nearly rode me off the road." He noticed the gun in Splinter's hand. "What's going on?"

"I wish I knew, sheriff," Splinter replied. As they went into the house he told him what had happened.

The two men sat down at the table, and Peanuts filled cups of coffee for them. Then he went back to his homework.

"Peanuts, what was in that hidin' hole?" Mulligan asked.

Peanuts looked up and grinned. "Just a couple of special marbles and an old pocket-knife Dad once gave me."

"Not much for a man to risk his life for."

"He was looking for something," Splinter said.

"Too bad Peanuts didn't hit him. We don't have much crime around here. I don't know how we'll ever find out who it was."

"We'll find out," Splinter said. "He'll be back to get what he was looking for."

The sheriff nodded. "I reckon you're right, Splinter. It must be something mighty important to do what he did."

"Important enough to murder for."

"Murder?"

Splinter nodded. "Hank Lane—remember? That was also a crime."

"Yeah, I haven't forgotten that. Do you think it could have been the same varmint?"

"Could be," Splinter replied. "Say, what brings you out here?"

"Oh, yeah." Mulligan took a deep breath. "I almost forgot. Judge Griffin came into town today and will be there for a couple days. He would like to see you both tomorrow afternoon after school is out."

Splinter nodded. "We can arrange that. Where will he be at?"

"My office," the sheriff replied, getting to his feet. "By the way, watch out for Bat Rogg. I hear he doesn't like bein' beaten at his own game."

CHAPTER THREE

WHILE Peanuts Lane washed himself and prepared for school, Splinter nosed around the stable and found a place to hide the money. When the boy came to get his pony, Splinter showed him what he had found.

"Loose manger," Peanuts said. "I was supposed to fasten it to the wall. Yeah, that'll be a good place."

"We'll leave it loose so we can pull it out when we want to get to the money. I think it's a good hiding place."

"Sure is, pard."

Peanuts saddled his pony and rode off to school. Splinter went into the house, wrapped the money in paper, and brought it down to the stable. He carefully dug out the dirt in the manger, placed the money in the hole and covered it, then shoved the manger back into place. He was dusting off his hands when he heard someone galloping into the yard.

Peanuts was riding in fast. He showered Splinter with dirt and gravel as he stopped his pony.

"The sheriff is dead!" Peanuts panted. "He's down the road a spell. I almost rode over him."

Splinter whirled and ran for his horse. It took him only a minute to saddle up, and then they rode off to investigate.

About halfway to Santa Nella they found the body of Irish Mulligan sprawled by the roadside. Peanuts remained mounted while Splinter quickly examined the officer. Then he looked up at the boy and said softly, "Ride into town and get his deputy."

"I'll do that. Then I'll go to school."

Someone had shot the sheriff in the chest. Splinter looked around but couldn't see the sheriff's horse. He wondered why anyone would want to kill the sheriff. Perhaps the bullet was intended for someone else. Thoughts popped into his mind. Could someone have thought it was Splinter McGee riding to town after the trouble last night at the Lazy L? Or did the masked man believe that the sheriff had recognized him, and had he wanted to make sure the officer would not tell?

Splinter was still considering the possibilities when Joe Walters and a couple of men arrived. They dismounted and looked down at the sprawled body.

"What a way to go!" Deputy Walters said. He turned to Splinter. "Peanuts said that Irish was out to your place last night."

"He was. Had coffee with us, then headed back to town. Peanuts found him this morning when he was riding to school."

"Heck of a thing for a kid to find," one of the men said.

"But why Irish?" Walters groaned. "What did he do to anyone? He was liked and respected by everyone."

Doc Hal Forbes came riding up in a wagon. He needed only a minute for his examination of the body.

"Shot through the heart," he said, shaking his head. Doc was short and heavy, with a fat, round face. He took out his handkerchief and wiped his forehead and face. "This is terrible, gentlemen," he added.

"Can we take him in now?" Walters asked.

"By all means. I understand the Lane boy discovered the body."

Splinter nodded. "He was on his way to school. He rode back to fetch me at the Lazy L."

The men lifted the body and gently placed it on the wagon. Then they all mounted while Doc turned the wagon around and headed for town. Walters drew back behind the others and said to Splinter, "Me and Irish been friends for many years. Neither has a relative, so we kinda took to each other. What am I going to do?"

"You're the sheriff now, and your first duty is to find the one who killed Mulligan."

"But Irish had the brains and I did the hard work. Right now I can't think straight."

"I know how you feel," Splinter said. "Let's wait till we get to town. Then we'll sit down and talk things over."

Santa Nella was up in arms over the murder of Sheriff Irish Mulligan. Word had spread, and by the time they brought the body back to town, everyone was gathered at the doctor's home. Joe Walters, still mounted, raised his hands for silence.

"This is a shock to everyone," he said as he leaned forward and rested his elbows on his saddle horn. "If anyone knows anything about Mulligan last night, come to the office and tell me. I'll need all your help in this matter."

"That and more," said a tall, well-dressed man. "We cannot tolerate such a crime."

Splinter eyed the man. He looked young, but there were deep lines in his face, showing he had undergone some rough times. He turned and spoke to some of the townspeople as they moved away.

"Who's that gent?" Splinter asked Walters.

"That's Al Harris. C'mon down to the office, McGee."

When they arrived there Joe Walters paused beside the desk and looked down at it. Splinter placed a gentle hand on his shoulders.

"It'll be tough for a while, Walters," he said.

Joe Walters sniffed and rubbed his eyes, then he shook his head.

"I just can't believe it, McGee. We been buddies for years—even before coming here.

This is our second term as officers. People respected Irish, so we didn't have too much crime. Only big thing was the murder of Hank Lane."

"I heard that Al Harris once robbed the bank here," Splinter said.

Walters nodded. "That was just before we were elected for the first term." He slowly rounded the desk and sank down in the chair. He looked up at Splinter. "I need help!"

Splinter said, "You'll get it, Walters. Now let's go over last night."

"I saw Irish right after supper, but I didn't know he left town. I was in the Glory Be, watchin' things. He slept at the Myers' home—had a room there. I thought this morning that he had overslept until Peanuts came riding in."

Splinter told Walters what had happened last night at the Lazy L. Walters said afterward:

"Do you suppose that masked man killed Irish?"

"Could be. He might have mistaken Mulligan for me riding in for help, or maybe he was afraid Mulligan had recognized him when he was making his getaway from the ranch."

"That sounds possible. But who can he be?"

"Are you willing to try and draw him out into the open?"

"I'd do anything to get him."

"Here's what you do—spread the word about what happened last night at the Lazy L. And let it slip that I'm positive I could identify the masked man if I saw him again, because of something he wore."

Joe Walters thought about it. "But, McGee, you'd be a walking target. I doubt if you'd live through this day." He shook his head. "I just couldn't do it."

"Suit yourself," Splinter said. "I was thinking of drawing the murderer out into the open."

"And then there's Peanuts. He'd be in danger too."

"Yeah, I forgot about him." Splinter sighed. "I'm used to playing a lone hand. Well, let's sit tight a day or two and see what happens. I've got to see Judge Griffin here this afternoon."

Splinter McGee spent the morning around Santa Nella, listening to people's opinions about the murder of the sheriff. He went from the Glory Be Saloon to the general store, then ended up at a small restaurant for noon dinner. He was joined at a table by Joe Walters.

"Funeral will be day after tomorrow, but in the morning the judge will hold an inquest, and he'd like you and Peanuts to be there."

"We'll be there—for both events."

"Got any new ideas?"

"Not yet."

"No one's come forth with anything." Walters sighed as he looked past Splinter and out through the front window. "Here comes the king and his men."

Splinter turned and looked. Coming down the middle of the street was King Ward followed by Bat Rogg and three other men. Splinter recognized Tad Wilson but not the other two. Walters told him they were Lippy Jones and Buzz Crocker.

"There goes a tough group," Walters said. "Any one of 'em would fight at the drop of a hat—and drop it themselves. I heard what you did to Rogg, and I'd be mighty careful around him. He's never been beaten before by anyone."

"Kinda the champion, eh?" Splinter chuckled. "He's got a lot to learn."

"Well, I wouldn't want him to learn at my expense."

"I'll try to be careful, but if he tries anything like he did yesterday, I might just forget being careful. Why didn't one of his men come to help him yesterday? That puzzled me."

Walters shrugged his shoulders. "Usually he doesn't need any help. Maybe they were celebrating at the bar and didn't know their champ was down and out."

"Do you know Tad Wilson?"

Walters shook his head. "I see him once in a while, but I don't know him. He's been here a short time. Took Zeke Brasil's place when he moved on to other pastures."

"Wilson spent time in Wyoming for rustlin'. I helped send him up. Yesterday he met me in the store just before I tangled with Rogg."

Walters grinned. "Tad probably told 'em about you, so he thought he'd bully you."

"I figured that out. But what Peanuts and I can't figure out is what that masked man was looking for at the ranch."

Joe Walters and Splinter were emerging from the restaurant when King Ward hailed them as he bowlegged his way toward them.

"What's this I hear about Irish Mulligan?" he asked Walters.

"Someone shot him last night between here and the Lazy L."

"Why aren't you looking for the killer?" Ward snapped.

"Maybe he's right here in town."

"Don't get smart with me, young feller."

"I ain't," Walters snorted. "If you don't like what I'm doing, mebbe you would like to be sheriff."

"If I was younger, I'd take you up on it."

"That seems to be the only thing you aren't running," Splinter said as he eyed the small cattleman.

"What's it to you?" Ward snapped. "I run this county."

"Maybe that's what's wrong with the county," Splinter said. As he turned and started away, Ward yelled out:

"You're not much of a detective!"

Splinter stopped, turned, and glared at the cattleman. Ward took a step backward. Splinter said, "Did you hear that from Tad Wilson? Well, did he also tell you that I helped send him up for cattle rustlin'?"

King Ward started to speak, but paused. Splinter continued:

"You might tell him—and your gang— that if they're doing anything wrong, I'll nail 'em, even if I'm not a range detective any longer."

"Not a detective any longer, eh?"

"I thought I deserved a rest, so I've been traveling for the past year. But once a detective, always a detective." Splinter turned and walked away.

"Why don't you get him to help you?" Ward asked Walters.

"I asked him, but he said he's got a job right now taking care of Peanuts and the Lazy L."

"I'll get him," Ward said. "You watch my smoke, Joe. You'll need help."

Splinter sat down on the shaded hotel porch and watched the people on the street. When school let out, he would meet Peanuts and they would go visit the judge.

He saw Ward and his four men ride out of town. They went past the hotel, but none of them gave him a glance. The sheriff's office was across the street, and he saw three businessmen go in. He wondered what they wanted.

* * *

Peanuts was standing beside his teacher's desk. Miss Skelly saw Splinter in the doorway, and she motioned for him to come in.

"I was just commending Jim for his fine work under the circumstances. I really don't know how he was able to do it in such a short time."

"He sure worked hard," Splinter said, removing his hat.

"I wish all my students took such interest. I believe that you have an appointment now with Judge Griffin. I have been asked to be present at the meeting."

"That's fine," Splinter said. "Let's close up the school and head for the sheriff's office."

Splinter assisted in closing windows and locking up, then he took Tina's books and carried them for her as they went outside. Peanuts unhitched his pony from a rack behind the school, led it up Main Street, and tied it beside Ranger.

They found Joe Walters, Judge Griffin, and Doc Forbes in the office. Walters introduced the judge to Splinter and Peanuts, then everyone sat down. The judge was tall and lean, with a stern expression and a large,

hooked nose. His white hair was long and
curly, and a lock fell over his forehead.

"This won't take but a few minutes," he
said. "As I understand it, Jim, your father
was killed and did not leave a will." He
paused, and Peanuts nodded. The judge continued: "Seeing that you are the only close
relative, there will be no problem. I have
legal papers here to be signed by myself and
three witnesses, giving you full possession of
the Lazy L ranch and whatever your father
left in the bank."

"Gee, that's great!" Peanuts exclaimed.

The judge turned to Splinter. "McGee, I
understand that you are staying at the Lazy
L. From what the late Sheriff Mulligan told
me, you and the young man are partners in
the ranch."

"Well, in a way, but not in owning anything," Splinter said. "You see, I'm just trying to help Peanuts get back on his feet. I
don't want to be any part of the ownership—
it's all his."

"We're pardners," Peanuts said. "What's
mine is yours."

"That's well and good, and I appreciate it,"
Splinter said, "but that's not what I want. I

want Peanuts to own everything, and I want to help him build up that ranch."

The judge nodded. "I understand, McGee," he said. "Mulligan told me about you, and I feel you'll be honest with the boy. But for a while he will need someone to watch over him and guide him in matters, so in this legal document it states that you are one of his guardians."

"Who else will there be?" Splinter asked.

"Miss Tina Skelly," the judge replied. "I feel a woman's touch may be needed at times. The two of you can work together, I am sure."

Splinter looked over at Tina, and she blushed.

"We'll do our best, judge," Splinter said.

"That's all the law can ask." The judge smiled as he shoved the document toward Joe Walters. "Walters, you and Doc Forbes can sign as witnesses to this arrangement. Then it will be legal."

The two men signed the document, then the judge rolled it up and said, "I'll file this in the courthouse right away. He rose to his feet. "McGee, you'd better check at the bank about the finances of the Lazy L."

After the judge and Doc Forbes had left the office, Walters told Splinter:

"They appointed me sheriff. And they suggested you be my deputy."

"I gave you my answer at dinner," Splinter said. "I've got my work cut out for me now."

As Tina reached for her books on the desk, Splinter quickly gathered them up.

"I'll see you home," he said. "We're going to have to get better acquainted now."

A minute later, Tina was walking between Splinter and Peanuts when they came face to face with Al Harris.

"Well, well! The teacher's got someone to carry her books," he said sarcastically.

"Please, Al," Tina said. "Mr. McGee and I have been appointed guardians for Jim Lane. We just left the judge, and we have some plans to work on."

"Oh, that's nice. Really, it's more than convenient."

Splinter handed the books to Peanuts, then took a step toward Harris.

"I wouldn't try anything," Harris snapped, his right hand spread above the butt of his six-shooter.

"I'm not—but you're asking for trouble, Harris. Just a little more and you'll find out that hell ain't full yet."

Harris's hand moved away from his gun.

He glared at them for a moment, then turned and crossed the street.

"I'm sorry," Splinter said to Tina.

"Why should you be? It was his fault. He's been looking for trouble ever since he came back."

Splinter relieved Peanuts of the books, and they continued to the rooming house where Tina Skelly lived. They sat down on the front porch.

"Where do we start?" Splinter asked.

"I think it best that you handle everything to do with the ranch, and I will take care of Jim's education. We can meet once or twice a week on any matter that we think needs the attention of both of us."

"That sounds good."

"Any financial matters can be handled by both of us," Tina added. "Do you know how the financial situation is at the Lazy L?"

"I reckon it's fine, but I'll check at the bank later."

"Perhaps you can send me a note by Jim in the morning, telling me what's in the bank. I presume he will need some clothing right away."

* * *

At the Santa Nella National Bank, Peanuts sat on the front steps while Splinter went inside. Henry Thomas, the owner, got up from his desk and motioned him to come over. He introduced himself and offered Splinter a chair.

"I've been waiting for you," he said as they sat down. "Judge Griffin was in earlier and said that you and Tina Skelly would be official guardians for Peanuts."

"That's right. Now I've got to find out how the Lazy L stands on your books."

"The Lazy L is in a comfortable position," Thomas replied as he picked up a ledger and opened it. "The Lane account has five thousand three hundred and forty dollars in it."

"That isn't bad. I believe we'll be able to get along on that for a spell."

"Henry Lane usually made a deposit by the tenth of every month," Thomas explained. "It was always a few hundred. Said it was payment on a business and building he had sold in Ohio. It's about due again, so when it comes, bring it in and I'll take care of it for you. Also, I'll notify the sender of Lane's death, and tell them to send the money to Peanuts."

"I'd appreciate that," Splinter said, getting to his feet. "This will make Peanuts happy. His supply of peanuts won't be cut off."

CHAPTER FOUR

THE inquest into the untimely death of Irish Mulligan drew people from all around the area. Even though Judge Griffin scheduled it for early morning, people began to arrive around seven o'clock and the two cafés in Santa Nella did a land-office business serving breakfasts.

Joe Walters was jumpy as he paced up and down in the sheriff's office, stopping now and then and looking out the doorway, hoping to see Splinter McGee. This was his first inquest, and he was uneasy about it.

Splinter and Peanuts Lane rode into town after breakfast at the ranch. As they came

down Main Street past the sheriff's office,
Joe Walters fairly flew out the door and
across the boardwalk, beckoning to Splinter.

"Am I glad to see you!" he sighed, nearly
out of breath. "I wanted to talk with you before the inquest."

Splinter grinned. "There's plenty of time.
Peanuts, take your pony down to the school
and tell Miss Skelly that you have to appear
in court for the inquest."

Peanuts rode on while Splinter dismounted
and tied his horse to the hitchrack. He followed Walters into the office.

"What am I going to do?" Walters wailed.

"It's not going to be that bad. In fact, the
judge will run about everything. All you'll
have to do is look smart and do as he orders.
And at the end, he'll ask that you find Mulligan's killer."

"That's it, huh?"

About five minutes later, Judge Griffin
was arranging some papers on his desk when
Splinter and Walters entered the courtroom.
He smiled and motioned them to come forward. The spectators' seats were nearly
filled. Walters stumbled on the wooden floor,
and Splinter grabbed him to prevent a fall.

"I'm glad to see you two," Judge Griffin said. "Where's our star witness?"

"He'll be here," Splinter said. "Had to check in at school first."

Walters sat down in a chair at a desk to the left of the judge's bench.

"This is going to be very simple," the judge said. "I'll call the witnesses and I'll select the jury. All you have to do, sheriff, is see that order is kept. I'll have McGee and Lane sit at that desk with you."

"Is that it?" Walters asked in a relieved voice.

"What did you expect?" the judge asked.

When Peanuts arrived, the judge directed him to the desk where the sheriff and Splinter were seated.

The judge opened the inquest by stating its purpose, and then he selected the jury from among the men residing in the area. Once they were sworn in and seated, he called on Peanuts Lane.

The boy gulped and looked at Splinter.

"Just tell 'em what you know," Splinter whispered as he patted the boy on the back.

After Peanuts was sworn in, the judge told him to tell the jury what had happened. Next

Splinter McGee took the stand, and finally Joe Walters.

Afterward, the judge asked the jury for their decision. The owner of the general store, acting as foreman, stood and announced, "Sheriff Irish Mulligan was killed by persons or person unknown. The law should do its utmost to apprehend the killer or killers."

The judge concluded the inquest, and people began to file out. Peanuts hurried back to school. The sheriff remained in his chair, staring at the wall. Splinter put a hand on his shoulder.

"It's all over now."

"All except apprehending the killer."

They were joined by King Ward, who asked Walters, "Have you selected a deputy yet?"

"Not yet. I just became sheriff. I need time to select a good man."

"Why not hire Buzz Crocker?"

"No, thanks," Walters said. "I'll select my own man."

"You need help and your friend here won't help you."

"I already have a big job," Splinter said. "If I can be of any help to the sheriff, I'll do what I can. But that's it."

"Talk that young one into selling me the Lazy L. Then you'll have time," Ward suggested.

"We're not selling to anyone. That's final!"

Splinter McGee walked along the main street, heading toward the hitching post in front of the sheriff's office. He was nearly there when someone called his name. Across the street, in front of the post office, the postmaster was waving to him.

"Glad I caught you," he said as Splinter came up on the walk. "Got a registered package for Henry Lane, but I don't reckon he'll be claimin' it. Seeing as how you're his son's guardian, I thought you could sign for it."

Inside the building, the postmaster went behind the counter and picked up a small package, about half the size of a shoe box and tightly wrapped.

"Sign here, McGee," he said, pointing to a line on a printed form.

Splinter signed, then picked up the package, which was from St. Louis.

"Lane received many such packages," the postmaster said. "Must be something he ordered."

All the way to the ranch, Splinter fingered the package, wondering what was in it. Did

Henry Lane buy things from some mail-order house in St. Louis? Splinter was still thinking about it as Ranger swung into the front yard. He happened to look up as a man stepped out of the house and fired at him.

Splinter dropped the package and reins and dived off his saddle, his hand snatching at his six-shooter. He fired once before the man dived behind the stable. He raised up, and the man fired at him, driving him back behind the brush.

After a minute, he scrambled to his feet and ran toward the stable. As he reached its doorway, he heard hoofs racing away. He ran to the corner of the stable in time to see a rider going up over the hill. Rushing across the yard, he entered the house and saw overturned chairs, bedding strewn all over the floor, pots and pans scattered, the stove almost taken apart, clothes scattered here and there.

"If I hadn't seen that fellow, I'd swear on a Bible that a cyclone hit here," he said as he surveyed the room. "What was he looking for?"

It was then that Splinter remembered the registered package, and he returned outside where Ranger was nibbling on the grass.

After a little search he found the package, and then, having taken care of Ranger, he went into the house and began to clean up.

The house was all in order by the time Peanuts came home from school accompanied by Tina Skelly. She was dressed in overalls, a flannel shirt, and high-heeled boots. Her hair was tucked up under her sombrero.

"Here's a telegram for you," she said, handing it to Splinter.

He opened it and slowly read it. He looked from Tina to Peanuts. "Darn that King Ward!"

"What has he got to do with it?" Tina asked.

"This is from the Cattlemen's Association. It says, 'McGee, request for you to assist new sheriff in Santa Nella by longtime member King Ward.'" He shook his head.

"I don't understand."

"I've worked on and off for the association," he explained. "One of Ward's riders knew me and told him, and he's been hounding me to help Walters. But I can't. I have my work here."

Splinter shook his head, then he told them what had happened to him when he returned from town. Tina was shocked, but Peanuts exclaimed, "We'll get 'em, pard. Must have been the same man as the other night."

"He's after something here. I wish we knew what it was," Splinter said.

"Do you think he's the man who killed the sheriff?" Tina asked.

Splinter shrugged. "Could be. That's why I have my work here. I want to help Peanuts get this ranch on an even keel."

"What about the telegram?" Tina said.

"I'll wire 'em refusing the job. I've done that before."

"Tomorrow morning's the funeral," Tina reminded him. "Afterward, perhaps, we can do some shopping for Peanuts."

"That's fine. He certainly needs a few things."

"Good. Well, I must be getting back to town. I'll see you both in the morning."

As she rode away, Splinter leaned against the porch post and watched her. Peanuts looked up at him and said, "She's sure nice, pard."

Splinter looked down at him and his face reddened. He nodded.

"I ain't goin' to tell anyone," Peanuts teased.

Inside the house, Splinter picked up the registered package and showed it to the boy.

"Did your Dad receive many of these?"

"I don't know. He could have and I never saw 'em."

Splinter removed the paper wrapping with care, so as not to destroy the return address. Under the wrapping was a tightly sealed box. Splinter cut the tape with his knife. Inside was currency! He handed it to Peanuts, who looked at it, then up at Splinter.

"More money!" the boy cried. "What's it all about?"

"I wish I knew." At the bottom of the box was a note. Splinter read it aloud:

"'Thanks, Lane. Price going up with your next shipment.'" Splinter squinted at the boy. "What shipment did your dad send to this St. Louis company?"

"I never knew Dad sent out anything. How much is in there?"

Splinter counted the large bills. "There's sixteen hundred dollars here."

"Golly Moses!"

"One puzzle on top of another." Splinter sighed as they put the box on the table and sat down. "What are we going to do with it?"

"Hide it with the other," the boy suggested.

"Good idea. Let's do it now before it gets dark and someone can sneak up on us."

He crossed the room and took a shotgun from a peg. After checking it carefully, he and Peanuts went to the stable. They stopped just inside the open doorway.

"You keep watch while I hide it," Splinter said, handing the shotgun to the boy. "Get behind that manger. If anyone comes in that doorway, tell 'em to stop, and if they don't— shoot."

Splinter quickly went to work, placing the money with the cache he had hidden previously. When he was finished, he took back the shotgun and they returned to the house.

"Watch out the window for a spell to see if anyone shows up," he told Peanuts. "Someone might have been watching us and wondered why we took a shotgun into the stable."

Peanuts drew up a chair by a window and watched. He was far enough back so it would be difficult for anyone outside to see him. He stayed there until supper was ready. Then he joined Splinter, who sat in a place at the table where he could see the stable through the window.

Nothing happened as darkness slowly crept over the land. Splinter wouldn't let Peanuts light the lamp, so they sat in darkness for nearly an hour before the moon appeared over the hill behind the stable.

"You can go to bed," Splinter said.

"Oh, no! Peanuts said. "I don't want to miss anything."

It was after ten when Peanuts finally gave up and turned in, but Splinter still sat in the chair by the window and watched.

As he watched, he slowly went over the events of the past week, starting with the shooting of Henry Lane. His mind was busy trying to figure out what was what, and how it all tied together. He was satisfied that Peanuts Lane was in a fine financial position and should anything happen to him, Splinter, he was sure that Tina Skelly would raise the boy.

Everything else went out of his mind as he thought about Tina. He had seen many attractive young women in his years, but she was the first one who really did something to him. Splinter chuckled softly. He had never seriously considered settling down—and here he was with a young boy to raise. The more he thought, the more convinced he became that Peanuts needed a mother to help raise him. What about Tina?

Suddenly his mind jerked back to reality as he thought he saw a shadow upon the stable. He hunched forward and withdrew his six-gun.

Again the shadow against the stable! Silently, a figure slithered past the front of it and went around a far corner.

Splinter ran outside and across the yard to the front of the stable, where he stopped.

He listened and heard a door opening. He slowly moved to the corner and peered around, but could see nothing.

Slipping into deeper shadows, Splinter made his way along the stable wall to the farther corner, which was near an old shed. As he came to the corner, he stopped, listened, then peeked around the corner.

The door of the shed was open. The moonlight was bright on this side of the stable and the shed. If he made a move, he might be seen. He was trying to figure out his next move when a figure appeared in the doorway. Splinter watched him as he stepped out and slowly closed the door.

"Hold it!" Splinter yelled as he stepped

away from the corner, his gun on the figure.

The man whirled, drawing and firing at the same time. The bullet whined past Splinter's head as he fired at the figure who darted around the shed.

Splinter dashed forward, but instead of going to the corner where the figure disappeared, he went down the other side of the shed to the rear, then stopped. He could hear someone running through the brush on the hill.

The shed was dark, with just a sliver of moonlight coming through the doorway. It was a room about eight feet square, but there was nothing in it. Splinter closed the door, listened for a moment, then started back toward the house.

Peanuts was standing by the door, and he grabbed Splinter about the waist as he came in.

"Gosh!" he gasped. "I heard shots."

"Someone came again, but I missed and he got away. He was investigating that old shed behind the stable."

"There's nothin' there."

"We're going to have to make sure of that," Splinter drawled.

CHAPTER FIVE

EVERYONE in the area turned out to pay their last respects to Irish Mulligan. The little white church building was packed, and people were standing around in the churchyard adjoining the church. Splinter, Peanuts, and Tina sat together. After a brief service at the grave, people began going back to town.

Later, Tina took Peanuts to the general store for some clothes while Splinter visited the sheriff's office, where he found Joe Walters tipped back in his chair, his boots up on the edge of the desk.

"That sure was hard," Walters said. "Took everythin' out of me."

"I reckon so," Splinter said, then added, "I got a telegram asking me to help you."

The sheriff looked puzzled. "How come?"

"Remember King Ward saying he'd get me? Well, he used the Cattlemen's Association, putting a little pressure on 'em, to make me help you."

"Will you?"

Splinter shook his head. "I told you I had a job—a mighty big job. I'm wiring the association today, telling 'em I can't." He went on to tell the officer what had happened the night before at the Lazy L.

"What can they be looking for?" Walters said.

"I wish I knew." Splinter sighed. "Someone knew yesterday that we'd be in here for the inquest, so they had plenty of time. But I'm puzzled about last night."

"I thought just about everyone was here yesterday."

"I've been thinking about it. As far as I can recollect, I never saw Bat Rogg, Tad Wilson, Al Harris, and a few others."

Walters thought about it, tugging at his mustache. "Yeah, now that you mention it, they wasn't there."

"Next time I hope I can wing whoever it is. That would at least put a mark on him."

"Funny it's all taking place at the Lazy L."

"Yeah, and it's only been in the last few weeks. Why not before that?"

"Say, that's right. Only problem Hank Lane ever had was turning away people who wanted to buy his ranch," the sheriff said.

"Why did they want that ranch?"

Walters shrugged his shoulders. "Only valuable thing is that spring back in the hills."

"Why did Lane purchase the place?"

"Said he liked Santa Nella, and old Windy Scott wanted to get away. So they made a deal. But Lane never really did too much there except build the ranch house and stable. Old Windy lived alone in one of them sheds."

"Was there more than one shed there?"

"Lane tore down one to build the house, but he left the other out behind the stable."

"What happened to Windy Scott?"

Walter shrugged his shoulders. "I don't know. Never saw him afterward. Reckon he took his money and pulled out."

"What about Al Harris?" Splinter asked.

"Al was here a long time ago. He had a

desire for money, so he robbed the Santa Nella National Bank. But he never got far. He was captured and sent up for five years."

"Did he get any money?"

"A few thousand, according to the bank, but it was never found." Walters laughed. "Maybe that's why he came back here."

"Could be. What does he do here in town?"

"Been doing some dealin' at the Glory Be," Walters said. "I think he's sore at you. He had a shine on Tina Skelly, and took her to several dances. But things seem to have changed since she and you became Peanuts guardians."

Splinter grinned as he rubbed his nose. "So that's it, huh? I've tried to figure out why he acted so unsociable when we met on the street. Shucks, I ain't cuttin' in on him."

The sheriff smiled. "I can tell that gal has eyes for you, McGee. And I watched you when she was around. Man, your eyes stuck out like the balls of a pawnshop."

Splinter shook his head. "She's a nice young lady, sheriff, but that's all."

At the depot Splinter filed his telegram of refusal to the Cattlemen's Association, and then, down the street, he entered the Glory

Be Saloon for a look around. The games were going full blast, and at the bar, King Ward, Bat Rogg, and Tad Wilson were talking with the sheriff. Ward motioned for Splinter to join them. As he approached, Rogg turned his back on him.

"Heard you turned down the association," Ward said.

"I told you I wasn't interested."

"Walters needs help, but he won't accept one of my men to be his deputy."

"I can't blame him." Splinter could see Rogg in the bar mirror, and Rogg was listening to every word.

"What's wrong with my men?" Ward growled.

"Plenty." Splinter replied.

That did it! Bat Rogg whirled around and clenched his fists.

"I thought you'd hear," Splinter said. "I saw your long ears twitching. They hear things they're not supposed to."

"Tryin' to be smart, eh?" Rogg grunted. He stepped past Ward to Splinter, eyeing him up and down.

"At least you're sober this time," Splinter said. "I hate to take advantage of a drunk."

"Drunk, eh? So you thought I was drunk

when you knocked me down? Well, this time I'll show you a thing or two."

"Stop before someone gets hurt!" Walters ordered, stepping in between the two men. But Rogg grabbed him and spun him around and back against the bar. Walters sagged as his spine struck the bar.

Rogg hadn't learned his lesson from his first meeting with Splinter, and he charged, both fists flaying away. But McGee side-stepped, and Rogg collided with several other men at the bar.

Rogg roared as he caught his balance and turned. He snorted, and charged again. This time Splinter held his ground, and as Rogg advanced he left his body wide open, and Splinter took advantage of the move and drove several hard rights and lefts into Rogg's chest and stomach. He took Rogg's blows on his shoulders, holding his ground.

The stomach blows took the wind out of Rogg for a second, but he gasped air and came back. This time Splinter quickly stepped to the left, and as Rogg came in he smashed him with a right fist to the face, flattening his nose. Blood spurted all over Rogg and the blow sent him back against the bar beside King Ward, who tried to stop him.

"You've had enough," Ward said, but Rogg jerked away and came back for more. This time Splinter one-twoed him on the chin, and he folded up and fell to the floor.

Splinter turned and stared at Ward and Tad, but neither man made a move. Joe Walters was leaning against the bar, a right hand on the butt of his six-shooter, watching them.

"Two times ought to make him realize he can't whip McGee," the sheriff said.

"He's stubborn," Ward said. Then he looked at McGee. "Watch out for him. I can't control his temper."

"I can take care of him," Splinter said as he took a deep breath.

"Next time it won't be with fists," Tad Wilson said. "He wanted to go gunnin' for you after the first beatin'."

"I'll welcome him any way he wants," Splinter said.

A few minutes later, he located Peanuts and Tina in the restaurant, where they were going to have their dinner.

"Wait till you see what I bought for Jim," Tina said. "I hope you approve. I spent fifteen dollars."

"I know I will—and don't worry about the money."

"I'm goin' to look real neat," Peanuts said. "Never had anythin' but overalls before."

"That's great." Splinter laughed, then looked at Tina. "How long have you been in Santa Nella?"

"I came here five years ago to teach school. Before that I taught in Phoenix."

"Was that before or after Harris was sent up?"

"After. I never met him until he returned. Why he came back I'll never know."

"Possibly to dig up the money he must have hidden right after the robbery," Splinter said. "That's the only reason I can think of."

"It could be," Tina said. "I went to several dances with him. He seemed so nice, but the other day I saw a different side to him. He asked me to go to tonight's dance, but I turned him down, and it upset him."

"I can imagine it would."

"There was nothing serious between us. Perhaps he believed there was."

"He'll get over it," said Peanuts, who had been listening intently. He looked at Splinter. "I asked Miss Skelly out to our ranch for supper, and maybe we could all take a nice ride."

"I accepted," she said.

Splinter grinned. "That's great. I've wanted to take a look at a spring behind the ranch. Maybe we can ride out there."

"I know how to get there," Peanuts said. "It's in the hills a little ways back of the house. I used to go out there with Dad to check the water."

An hour later the three of them rode out of Santa Nella. Tina had changed her clothes, and Splinter had picked up the packages at the general store. They dropped off the packages at the ranch house, then Peanuts led the way into the hills.

The spring was in a small valley at the foot of a rocky hill. There were some big trees around the spring, and several head of cattle were drinking there as the trio rode up. Splinter pointed to the cattle, all branded Lazy L.

"We have some livestock, pardner," he said. "Hope there's more on the ranch."

"There should be fifty head in all," Peanuts said. "Dad and I made a count a couple months ago."

They dismounted and looked around. Tina sat down on the ground while Splinter picked up a broken branch and poked it into the water, stirring it up. Peanuts watched him closely.

"Looks fine," Splinter said as he knelt down at the edge of the water and scooped some of it up in his cupped hands. He tasted it. "Tastes fine too."

"This is the water everyone wants," the boy said.

"It's the best water in the valley," Tina said. "Some have said that Henry Lane was killed over it."

"That's possible." Splinter nodded. "Men will kill for good water."

"After they can't buy it," Peanuts added wisely.

Splinter nodded again as he looked off to the jagged rocks on the hill.

"Probably a good view from up there," he said.

"You can see the ranch from there. I went up there once, but Dad told me never to go up again. He was awful mad at me and hit me. I think it's the only time he ever did that."

"Did he say why he did it?" Tina asked.

Peanuts shook his head. "Nope. I reckon he had a reason."

"I wonder what his reason was," Splinter said.

They sat down beside Tina and talked, but Splinter remained puzzled as to why Henry Lane didn't want his son to climb that hill. Young boys liked to climb hills and look things over. Even older men at times had that urge. Right now Splinter McGee had that urge.

"How about us three climbing to the top of that hill?" he said.

Peanuts looked thoughtful. "Maybe I shouldn't."

"I think it would be all right," Tina said.

Splinter got to his feet, took Tina's hand, and helped her up. They stood and looked at each other until Peanuts stepped between them.

"C'mon," he said as he hurried forward.

At times the climb was steep, and Splinter assisted Tina, holding her arm and taking her hand. She always smiled at him and thanked him. Reaching the top, they halted to catch their breath and to look out over the valley and the Lazy L ranch.

"What a lovely view," Tina said.

"That's what I thought," Peanuts agreed, "but I reckon Dad thought differently."

They began to walk in and out of the large boulders. Peanuts got tired of just walking, so he climbed up on the boulders and leaped from one to the other until he was a little distance ahead of them.

"Hey!" he screamed suddenly, jumping up and down, waving his arms.

"What's the matter?" Tina exclaimed.

Splinter hurried through the boulders toward where Peanuts was still jumping up and down.

"Lookee! Lookee!" the boy yelped, pointing down between two of the boulders. Splinter rounded the boulder and stopped.

Down between the two boulders was a skeleton. It looked as if it had been shoved down there. There was also, half burned in the dirt, parts of two boots, a cartridge belt, and a six-shooter.

Splinter shook his head at the sight. "He's been dead for a long spell."

"Who is it?" Tina asked as she peered around Splinter.

"That's going to be hard to tell."

Splinter studied the remains for several minutes, then put his handkerchief atop the boulder, holding it in place by a large rock. Then he joined Tina and Peanuts.

"This is terrible. I'm so sorry you two had to see that skeleton."

"It's my first one," Peanuts said. "Gee, what a thing to look down at."

Splinter sighed. "We have to notify the sheriff and let him take charge. I'll ride in and fetch him."

"I'll stay with Peanuts at the ranch," Tina said. "Perhaps we can fix supper together."

"Gee, that would be great," Splinter said.

Splinter found Joe Walters in the Glory Be and told him of the discovery. They rounded up Doc Forbes and headed for the Lazy L. It was easy to get to the foot of the hill, but from there on they had to travel on foot. Doc brought along a canvas bag to carry the skeleton back to town.

Doc Forbes stared at the skeleton before his examination. "Looks like he was dead and then shoved down in between these two boulders," he said.

Walters carefully picked up the six-shooter and shoved it inside the waistband of his pants.

After the examination, Doc Forbes asked the other men to help place the skeleton inside the canvas bag.

"Has he been here long, Doc?" Walters asked.

"Quite a few years."

"Going to be hard to tell who it was," Splinter said.

"That it is," Doc Forbes agreed.

Splinter entered the opening that the skeleton had occupied and ran his fingers through the sand repeatedly. Finally he found a bullet. He held it up so the officer and doctor could see it.

Doc shook his head. "Can you imagine that! A bullet! Perhaps the one that killed this man."

"It sure could be," Splinter said as he handed it to Walters. "Better hang on to it, sheriff. It's a little evidence."

"Looks like a .38 caliber," Walters said.

They carried the canvas bag to the wagon, and Splinter left them as they swung past the Lazy L ranch house. Tina and Peanuts were on the front porch and waved to the men.

When Splinter walked into the house, he could see a difference. The old place had been cleaned and straightened up and the table was set, ready for evening supper. He stood in the doorway with a smile on his face.

"Like it, pard?" Peanuts asked.

"It doesn't look like the same place."

Splinter turned to Tina. "Gee, I don't know how to thank you."

"I don't need any thanks." Tina smiled. "It was fun. I haven't had a place that I could do anything with for many years."

"Well, come out more often," Splinter said, grinning.

Peanuts led him over to the table and pointed to his place. "You sit here, pard," he said.

Tina served a meal fit for a king, and Splinter and Peanuts ate to their heart's content.

"Ain't ate anything like this since my ma cooked, and that was long ago," Splinter said.

"Do you still remember her cookin'?" Peanuts asked.

"Yeah. That was before the Indians raided the town and killed my ma and pa."

While Peanuts cleared the table, Tina opened her purse and brought out some papers.

"These are the bills for Peanuts' new clothes," she told Splinter. "He asked me to call him Peanuts."

"That's mighty fine."

She spread the papers out on the table.

"This is for six new shirts," she explained, pointing to one of the papers.

Splinter leaned forward, his right hand on the back of her chair. Their faces were only inches apart. Splinter glanced quickly toward Peanuts, then back to Tina. The boy was washing dishes in a large tub, his back to them.

"Six shirts?" Splinter said. "I never owned more than one at a time."

Tina smiled as she looked intently into his face. "You should have a few new things too," she said.

Splinter shook his head. "I can get what I need when I need it."

"Oh, I wasn't expecting to take *you* shopping," Tina said, a sparkle in her eyes. She turned back to the papers, pointing to another one. "This is for a new suit. I thought he should have something besides overalls."

"I agree," Splinter said.

"Wait'll you see me in that new suit!" Peanuts said as he turned around from his work. 'It's a dandy, pard."

"These are other things he needed badly," Tina said to Splinter. "I'm sure you understand."

They leaned forward a little more, till their

faces were within inches of each other. Suddenly Tina moved forward and kissed his cheek. Then she pulled back and turned to the papers before her.

Splinter smiled. He wasn't sure about Tina before, but now he was.

"Thanks for taking care of everything," he said softly.

"It's been a pleasure," she said, not looking up at him.

Peanuts turned from his work. "I'm finished here," he said.

"I think you should check our horses before we ride into town with Tina," Splinter suggested.

"You don't have to ride back with me," Tina said.

"I insist," Splinter said. "Especially since so many things have been happening around here."

Peanuts went out the door, leaving them facing each other. Splinter smiled, and Tina looked at him seriously.

"You look like the little boy who had just won the prize," she said.

"I don't know what I've won, but life has been awful good lately."

He took a step forward, paused, and she

came in close, and his long arms slowly encircled her. He looked down into her pretty face. There was a twinkle in her eyes, then she closed them as their lips met. It was a long kiss. Finally it ended, but he held her tight and her body shuddered slightly as she held on to him.

Their sweet moment of bliss ended when Peanut called out: "Horses are ready!"

Splinter and Tina looked at each other, quickly snatched another kiss, then walked to the doorway, where they looked out. Peanuts had all three horses and was leading them to the front.

It was just getting dark when they rode into town. There was a big crowd in town for Saturday night. Off Main Street, in a hall, a three-piece orchestra was warming up for the monthly dance.

"I've gone to some of the dances," Tina said, "and they always end up in a brawl."

They dismounted near Tina's rooming house.

"I'll take Miss Skelly's horse and put it in the stable out back," Peanuts said.

Tina and Splinter walked up the wooden walk to the front porch. There was a lamp burning in the living room, and the front door was open.

"I believe Mrs. Anderson is in the house," Tina murmured.

"I understand. Well, I want to thank you for a grand day. I'm sorry about the skeleton."

"It's certainly been a grand day." She took his hand. "We must do it again."

"All but the skeleton part."

They both laughed as they heard Peanuts returning. Tina hugged the boy, then looked up at Splinter, wishing she could do the same to him.

They left her and rode back to Main Street. Sheriff Joe Walters was standing on the sidewalk, and he waved to them.

"Find out anything about the skeleton?" Splinter asked.

Walters shook his head. "Nope. It's even got King Ward shakin' his head."

They turned their horses out into the middle of the street and rode out of town. As they left town, Splinter said to the boy, "Let's fan leather home, pard!"

And that they did, reaching the ranch in record time. They rode into the stable and quickly dismounted and unsaddled their horses. Splinter stopped Peanuts from running to the house.

"Just wait a minute," he said. "It's so quiet out here. Let's be careful."

Splinter drew his gun and they walked slowly toward the house. As they stepped up on the front porch, they both stopped short. Fastened on the door was a piece of paper with something written on it. Splinter glanced around, then pulled the paper off the door, pushed the door open, and went in, Peanuts quickly closing the door behind them.

"Wait a minute—don't light the lamp yet," Splinter said.

They waited, listening, but they couldn't hear a thing. Finally Splinter struck a match and looked around. The room was in order, so he went to the table and lit the lamp.

"What was that on the door?" Peanuts asked.

Splinter opened the paper and looked at it. It read: *GET OUT OR DIE*.

CHAPTER SIX

SUNDAY morning found two bleary-eyed residents at the Lazy L. The note had shaken them up and it had been difficult for them to sleep.

"Why is someone tryin' to get us out of here?" Peanuts asked as they finished breakfast.

"I sure wish I had the answer." Splinter shoved his chair back and looked at the boy. "Think hard, pardner—did your father ever mention anything that could lead to this?"

Peanuts scratched his head, thinking. Finally he shook his head. "I know that King

Ward and Al Harris both wanted to buy the ranch, but I don't think either of 'em would murder for it."

"There's got to be something besides that water spring."

"That's all I ever heard 'em talkin' with Dad about."

Splinter wasn't satisfied with that answer. He got up and went out on the porch. Everything seemed serene, but he wondered if anyone was watching the ranch.

Peanuts joined him in a few minutes.

"No one in sight," Splinter said.

"Uh-huh. Maybe they're in church this mornin'."

"Say, that's right—it's Sunday. I forgot." Splinter looked down at Peanuts. "Do you go to church?"

The boy shook his head. "Dad never went," he replied. "But Miss Skelly goes to church."

"I suppose she does. She's a good woman."

"What are we goin' to do?"

Splinter nodded. "Yeah, what are we going to do? 'Get out or die!' Not a very promising future."

"I say we stay," the boy said firmly.

"Let's sit tight and see what happens," Splinter suggested. "No use going to the sheriff with more problems. We'll wait till afternoon, and then we'll ride into town and see what we can find out."

They worked about the place, but their hearts were not in their work, and they continually scanned the hills back of the stable.

It was after dinner when they spotted a lone horseman coming down the road toward the ranch house. Splinter kept Peanuts inside as he stood in the doorway and watched the approaching rider.

As the rider swung into the yard, they saw it was King Ward. He was dressed in his Sunday clothes, with no gun visible. They stepped out on the porch as he drew rein and dismounted.

"Howdy," Splinter greeted him. "Nice to see you, Ward."

The old cattleman grunted as he climbed up on the porch. "Nothin' nice about me comin' out here, McGee."

"Well, it's just in the way you look at it."

Ward accepted a chair. Splinter sat in the other chair, and Peanuts on the top step.

"Why do you defy me?" Ward asked gruffly.

"I ain't defying you. I've got a job to do."

"I know that, but you could help Walters out. He's going round in circles now that he has three dead men to account for. Why don't you sell this ranch and move into town? Then you could help him."

Splinter looked sharply at the old rancher. Then he turned to the boy. "Peanuts, get that note."

A minute later, Ward's eyes widened as he read the note. "Where'd you get this?" he asked.

"Fastened to our front door last night," Splinter said. "Know anything about it?"

Ward's eyes narrowed as he tossed the note to the floor. "Are you accusing me of sending it?" he demanded.

"Someone did—someone who wants this ranch."

"And because I want this ranch you thought—Heck, man, I wouldn't do anything like that. I've always been in the open in all my deals."

"Why do you want this ranch?"

"I need that water," Ward replied gruffly.

"It's more than just water," Splinter snapped. "Now, what is it?"

"Nothing else," Ward replied, getting to his feet. "That spring would solve a lot of my problems."

"I don't think that water is a killin' matter.

Yet it looks that way because no one knows
any other reason for wanting this ranch."

Ward stepped to the edge of the porch, then
turned back.

"I'll meet any price you put on the place,"
he said. "I'll give you one week to—"

His knees jerked as the report of a rifle
echoed off the hills. He stumbled forward and
Splinter caught him in his arms.

"Blast him!" Ward muttered.

"Blast who?" Splinter asked quickly. But
Ward didn't answer. His face twisted with
pain and he closed his eyes. Splinter
stretched the cattleman out on the porch and
looked at Peanuts.

"Pardner, saddle up and get the Doc and
the sheriff as fast as you can—and watch out
for an ambush!"

"I'll make it." Peanuts stepped over the
fallen man and raced for the stable.

Splinter squinted at the hills behind the
stable, but he couldn't see any movement. He
looked down at King Ward, wondering what
he had meant by his words, "Blast him!"

About an hour later Peanuts returned with
Sheriff Walters, Bat Rogg, and Tad Wilson.
The doctor was coming behind them in a
wagon. They mounted the porch and looked

at Ward, who was breathing heavily and groaning.

"Thank God he's alive," Walters said to Splinter. "What happened?"

"And tell the truth!" Rogg added through swollen lips. His nose was still black and blue from their fight.

As Splinter ended his narrative to the sheriff, Doc Forbes arrived in his wagon. He grabbed his black case from the seat and waddled his way up on the porch, shoving Wilson and Rogg to one side.

"He's still alive," he said as he got down on his knees beside the victim.

"That took a lot of medical knowledge," Wilson grunted.

Doc glanced up at the cowboy, then went on with his examination. He turned Ward on his side and looked at his back where the bullet had struck. Then he lowered him again.

"Nasty wound," he said to Splinter. "Got some hot water and something we can use for bandages?"

There was hot water in a pot left from their dinner. Splinter took a clean sheet from a shelf and carried it and the water out on the porch. By then the doctor had pulled off Ward's coat and shirt. He used some pieces of the sheet to bathe the wound, then he carefully wrapped him up tight.

"He'll survive," he said, getting to his feet. "Will one of you get that blanket in my wagon so we can transport him back to town?"

Wilson fetched the blanket. They rolled up Ward and transferred him to the wagon. Doc climbed up on the seat and started off. Wilson and Rogg mounted their horses and followed, but the sheriff stayed behind.

"Thought we could check on some things," he said to Splinter.

"What's on your mind, sheriff?"

"Why would anyone want to kill King Ward?"

Splinter shrugged his shoulders. "That's a good question. I been doing a lot of thinking about it. I'll tell you something I wouldn't say before Doc and those others. Ward muttered 'blast him' just after he was hit. Made me wonder if he knew someone was out to get him, or if he ordered someone to get me, and they got him by mistake."

"He said that, eh?" Walters scratched his head. "Things seem to go from bad to worse."

"They sure do." Splinter removed the warning from his pocket and handed it to

Walters. "Peanuts and I found this fastened to the door when we came home last night."

"Just goes to prove what I just said—from bad to worse." The sheriff shook his head as he handed the note back.

"I've been scratchin' my head on this one," Splinter said. "It all seems to be centered on the Lazy L."

"It can't be this ranch," Peanuts said after listening to the two men. "It was so nice and peaceful for so long. Dad and I loved it here."

"If we only knew what someone was after," Splinter said.

"Water?" Peanuts asked.

"It's more than that," the sheriff replied. "But getting back to King Ward—who knew he was coming out here? I saw him in church. Right afterward he pulled out. I thought he was heading home."

"Someone may have followed him. Or they were waiting out there for me to go to the stable where they'd have a clear shot at me," Splinter said. "When he stood on the edge of the porch, they might have taken Ward for me. But we're not at all the same size."

Walters moved over to where Ward had stood. "That bullet hit him just below his right shoulder," he said, measuring with his hands. He turned and looked off toward the hills. "Must have been about halfway up that hill in the brush."

Splinter squinted at the hill and nodded.

"Let's take a look out there," the sheriff suggested.

Splinter and Peanuts followed him across the yard, past the stable, and up the side of the hill. After a while he stopped and looked back toward the ranch.

"He was around this spot," Splinter said. "Let's spread out and search the ground for any signs."

The sheriff moved on up while Splinter moved to the right and the boy went to the left. They moved slowly, searching the ground. Suddenly Peanuts let out a yelp, and the two men hurried over to him where he was jumping up and down and waving his hands in the air so that they could see him in the heavy brush.

"Lookee here!" he said, pointing just ahead of him to a small opening in the heavy brush. There were footprints, several cigarette butts, and one rifle shell that glistened in the sunlight.

"This is the spot," the sheriff declared. "They sure left a lot of evidence."

"This proves they didn't follow King Ward from town," Splinter said as he watched the sheriff move carefully into the opening and kneel down to pick up the shell and the cigarette butts.

"From the looks of it, he waited here for a long spell," Walters said.

"When you saw Ward in church, were any of his men there?"

The sheriff shook his head. "I don't think any of 'em ever stepped inside a church. They never even went into the church to pay their last respects to Irish."

"Were Rogg and Wilson in town when Peanuts rode in to get you?"

Walters scratched his head and tugged at his mustache, thinking deeply. "By golly! They were just riding into town as I went for my horse."

They took a final look around, then walked back down the hill to the ranch house. The sheriff thanked them for their help before returning to Santa Nella.

Splinter and Peanuts sat down on the porch.

"What next?" the boy asked.

"I wish I knew," Splinter replied. "This

mystery seems to get more involved every few hours."

"Wish I could help you."

"You've been a mighty big help so far. How'd you like to take a ride?"

Peanuts nodded.

"Saddle up our horses," Splinter said. "I'll get a few things to take along."

Peanuts got to his feet and headed for the stable. Splinter went into the house, where he removed two rifles and checked to see that they were loaded. He came back to the front door just as Peanuts came out of the stable leading Ranger and his small pony.

"Goin' huntin'?" Peanuts asked with a smile.

"Might," Splinter replied. "Thought we ought to be prepared just in case we ran into anything."

He slid the rifles into the scabbards on their saddles. Then he took the rope off his saddle.

"I'll be back in a second," he said as he went back into the house.

Peanuts mounted and patted the rifle. It was the first time he had ever ridden with a rifle on his saddle. It thrilled him. He waited

for Splinter to come out. Splinter appeared
from around a corner of the house. He swung
into his saddle and headed out past the stable
with Peanuts following.

"What'd you do with your rope?" the boy
asked.

"Just fastened the door shut tight in case
someone tries to get in. The window's easy to
enter, but hard to get out of in a hurry."

"Where are we goin'?"

"Out to the spring, and then do a little investigating up among those boulders where
you found the skeleton yesterday."

"Think we missed somethin'?"

"You never can tell."

They galloped down through a narrow ra-
vine and then up a hill and into the small
valley where the spring was located. They
rode their horses up the side of the hill as far
as they could, then dismounted and tied them
to a tree.

"Better take your rifle with you," Splinter
said as he slipped out his own.

Peanuts wished for some action as he fingered the rifle. His father had taught him
how to use it, but he had fired it only at tin
cans. He looked up at Splinter, admiration in

his eyes as he followed him up to the boulders.

"Climb up on top of that tall boulder and keep watch," Splinter said. "And don't let anyone sneak up on us."

Peanuts did as instructed, sitting down on the boulder. From there he could see all over the area.

"Don't see a thing," he called out to Splinter, who was sifting through the dirt where the skeleton had lain for so many years.

Time passed swiftly as both were occupied with their duties. From time to time Peanuts got to his feet, stretched, took a long look around, then sat down. He was getting tired and craved some action.

Splinter, intent on his work, didn't notice the passing of time. He was covering every inch of the area. Suddenly his fingers felt something in the dirt. Carefully he brought out an old ring. It was a man's ring of hammered silver, with a turquoise.

"C'mon down!" he called out to Peanuts.

The boy slid down off the boulder and joined him.

"Ever see that ring before, Peanuts?"

The boy looked closely at it and thought for a while. "I remember it, pard, but I can't remember where I saw it—or who had it."

"Maybe this will help us identify the skeleton. Reckon we better head home now."

The ranch was quiet as they rode in, stabled their horses, and went to the house.

"We have to use the window," Splinter said. "We'll just keep the door tied shut."

He boosted Peanuts across the windowsill and followed. He lit several lamps and began to prepare supper.

"I keep thinkin' about that ring," Peanuts said. "I know I saw it somewhere."

"Keep thinking. Let's make it a game—a thinking game. If we think hard enough, we'll find an answer or two."

"Ring, ring—whose ring?" Peanuts sang.

"I'll take it into town in the morning and see if anyone recognizes it."

"Will you ride in with me when I go to school?"

"Sure. Let's pray tonight that we get an answer tomorrow."

CHAPTER SEVEN

SANTA Nella was just waking up as they rode down Main Street. Except for the youngsters heading for school, there was very little activity. Peanuts headed for the school while Splinter reined in at the hitchrack in front of the sheriff's office. When he discovered that the office was still closed and locked he sauntered across the street to the general store. Ira Crabb was just coming out.

"Fine morning," Splinter said as he took the ring from his pocket and showed it to Crabb. "Have you ever seen this ring before?"

The lawyer took the ring and examined it.

"It does look familiar. Where did it come from?"

"I found it," Splinter replied. "Thought possibly it might belong to someone and that he'd want it back."

Ira Crabb nodded slowly as he handed the ring back to Splinter. "There's something about it that seems familiar, but I'm not sure. I'll think about it, and if the owner comes to mind, I'll inform you."

"That's fine." Splinter grinned as he went into the store. Crabb walked slowly down the street, stroking his chin.

"Never saw it before," Andy Anderson, owner of the store, declared. "'Course, I'm not partial to rings, so I wouldn't pay that close attention."

"What about a ring?" Ma Anderson asked as she came from the rear of the store. She took the ring and looked at it.

"Handmade," she said. "Let me see. I remember someone coming in here who had a ring just like that. Oh, goodness me! That was years ago. He used to buy a lot of things here."

"Are you sure, Ma?" Anderson asked.

She nodded. "Let me think." She handed

the ring back to Splinter. "I'll think of who owned it."

"Just let me know—or the sheriff," he said.

After leaving the store Splinter walked up the street to the hotel. The lobby was empty, but a clerk was dusting off the counter.

"Howdy, McGee. What can I do for you?"

"You been here a long time?"

"See those hills yonder? Well, they was gopher mounds when I first came to Santa Nella."

"That's a long time, pardner."

"I know all the history of this little town. What do you want to know?"

The clerk looked at the ring, studied it, tossed it up and down in his hand, looked at it again, then handed it back to Splinter.

"Yep. I seen it—but a long time ago," he said, scratching his neck thoughtfully. "Let me see. Was it—Nope, it wasn't. He never wore a ring. Dang it, McGee. I know but I don't know—if you know what I mean."

"You remember the ring, but you're not sure who wore it?"

"That's it. Wish I could come to the point like that."

"What ring?" a voice asked.

They turned to see Al Harris coming down the stairs.

"Selling a ring?" he asked. "I buy old rings."

"This one isn't for sale," Splinter said. "I'm trying to find the owner."

"Let me see it. I may be able to help you."

Having examined the ring, Harris shook his head and handed it back to Splinter. "Nice ring, but not worth too much," he said. He turned and walked out of the lobby.

"Al Harris likes rings and other jewelry," the clerk said.

"Does he live here at he hotel?"

"Ever since he came back. Works at the Glory Be as a gambler. Good man."

"I'll bet he pays his bill on time."

"How'd you know?"

Splinter chuckled as he turned and walked out of the hotel. He stood on the walk for a moment, then returned to the sheriff's office. The door was open now, and Sheriff Walters was sitting at his desk with some papers.

"What's this I hear about a ring?" he asked.

"Found it late yesterday out where we

found the skeleton." Splinter handed the ring to the officer.

"I've never seen it before. I better keep it."

Splinter nodded. "I came earlier, but you weren't here, so I thought I'd see if anyone recognized it. Got a little interest from Ira Crabb, Mrs. Anderson, and the hotel clerk. They seem to recall seeing it once but can't place it with a person—so far."

"Ma Anderson's sharp," Walters said. "She'll come up with an answer. Do you think it belonged to the skeleton?"

Splinter nodded. "Otherwise, how would it get way out there between those boulders?"

Doc Forbes came through the open doorway, and he said to Splinter at once, "King Ward's conscious, and he wants to talk to you."

"How's he doing?"

"Pretty fair, I'd say. He gained consciousness just a while ago, and right away asked for you. Said I'd see if you were in town. He said you'd better be."

"He's better already," the sheriff said. "Mind if I come along?"

"Glad to have you," Splinter said.

"I don't believe Mr. Ward would be glad—

at least for the present," Doc Forbes said. "He said specifically that he wanted McGee alone."

"Come on, anyhow," Splinter said quickly. "This might be interesting."

They hurried to the doctor's house, and Splinter placed the sheriff in the hallway just outside Ward's room. Splinter entered, but he left the door ajar slightly.

King Ward was lying on his right side. He turned his head slightly to look at Splinter.

"Get over here," he ordered gruffly, and pointed to the chair next to the bed.

"How are you doing?" Splinter asked.

"Bad!" the old rancher grunted. "What day is this?"

"Monday morning."

"Doc bandaged me up like a Christmas package. Can't move!"

"You're lucky to be alive."

Ward eyed Splinter. "Did you see who shot me?"

Splinter shook his head. "Nope. It was done from the hills behind the stable. Do you know who did it, Ward?"

The old rancher's eyes narrowed for a moment, then closed as he shook his head slowly. "How should I?"

"You said right after you were shot, 'Blast him!' "

The old man thought about it. "Funny what you'll say at a time like that."

"We found the spot where the shot was fired from. And an empty 30-30 shell. The sheriff was with us."

Ward moved slowly, trying to get into a more comfortable position. "I went out there to make an offer for your ranch—nothin' more."

"Well, me and Peanuts talked it over, and we put a price on the Lazy L."

"How much?"

"Two hundred and fifty thousand."

"That ranch ain't even worth the twenty thousand I offered Hank Lane."

Splinter grinned. "I reckon we're a long ways apart, Ward. Is there anything else you want to talk with me about?"

Ward glared at Splinter as he got to his feet.

"I'll talk with you plenty when I get out of here," he growled.

"Fine." Splinter walked out of the room and closed the door behind him.

The sheriff was leaning against the wall. He shook his head and followed Splinter into

the front room of the house, where Doc
Forbes was talking to Bat Rogg. The foreman
eyed Splinter and the officer, then turned to
the doctor.

"What's he doin' in there with the boss?"

"Ward asked for him," the doctor replied.

Rogg looked at Splinter. "I don't believe
your story about the shooting. I think you
shot King Ward."

"Well, mister, you'd better talk it over with
your boss. He'll straighten you out mighty
quick—or I will again!"

Rogg said to the doctor, "I'll see the boss
now."

"I'll see if he's up to talking with anyone
else." Doc Forbes turned and went down the
hall.

"That's a crazy way to run things!" Rogg
grumbled.

The doctor came back shaking his head.
"Ward said he doesn't want to see anyone for
a while. He wants to rest and think."

"Well, I'll be darned!" Rogg snapped. He
whirled and rushed out of the house.

"Funny that Ward didn't want to talk with
Rogg," Doc said. "He's strong enough."

In another minute Splinter and the sheriff
also left the doctor's house.

"If King Ward doesn't get well fast, Bat Rogg'll ruin the Box W," Walters said as they walked toward his office.

"If Ward died, who would take over the ranch?" Splinter asked.

Walters stopped on the edge of the walk, looking down at the dirt for a moment, then he half turned to Splinter. "That's a good question, Splinter. I doubt if anyone ever gave any thought to that."

"King Ward ain't going to live forever. Has he got any relatives?"

"I don't know."

"Maybe your esteemed lawyer would know."

"Ira Crabb, eh? Well, he might have an idea, but he'd charge you to hear it." The sheriff chuckled. "I'd better have a little chat with him."

A voice called out from across the street, and then the two men saw Ma Anderson hurrying toward them.

"That ring," she panted. "I knew I'd seen it. It belonged to Windy Scott."

"Are you shore of that, Ma?" the sheriff asked.

"I'd swear to it on a stack of Bibles," she replied. "He used to visit the store, and he always wore that ring. I can see it just as plain as anything."

"Windy Scott, eh?" Walters cuffed his hat down over one eye and looked at Splinter. "He used to own the Lazy L before Hank Lane bought it from him."

"We sure thank you, Mrs. Anderson," Splinter said. "It's nice to have a citizen who's interested in helping the law."

She beamed all over as she turned and hurried back across the dusty street. The two men entered the office, and Walters sank down in his chair while Splinter leaned against the desk and looked down at the officer.

"Windy Scott," the officer grunted. "We always wondered where he went."

"How long after the sale did he disappear?"

Walters shook his head. "I was working then at the Box W and didn't see people in town too much. I heard people talk about it, and some said he said he was going East to celebrate."

"Looks like he didn't go East."

"That skeleton—do you suppose...?"

Splinter nodded. "It's our best bet right now."

"Well, that clears up one mystery."

"You better tell Doc so he can make the arrangements," Splinter said. "Do you have any idea who was in on the sale?"

"Henry Thomas might know. It was probably done at the bank."

"I'll see him while you tell Doc," Splinter said.

Henry Thomas looked up from his desk as Splinter stepped into his office. His face broke into a beaming smile.

"Is there something I can do for you, McGee?"

"You've probably heard about the skeleton we found Saturday. Well, we're almost sure now that it's Windy Scott."

Thomas looked amazed. He shook his head. "Are you sure?"

As Splinter told him about the ring, Thomas nodded.

"I recall Scott wearing a turquoise ring. In fact, he said that he had made it himself. Why, this is terrible! Windy Scott! He never hurt anyone. When he got his money for the ranch, he said he'd be heading East."

"He never made it," Splinter said. "Who was here at the time that he received his money?"

Thomas rubbed his chin thoughtfully, his eyes partly closed as he considered the question.

"That was a long time ago," he said slowly. "I know I was here with Henry Lane and Scott. But there was someone else. King Ward was here, and so was Al Harris. Ward was trying to get Scott to sell to him, but Scott hated Ward and wouldn't take his offer. Harris happened to be in the bank at the time. That was just prior to his trying to empty our vaults."

"Did you handle the legal paperwork?"

"I did. Ira Crabb was away at the time, so he gave the papers to me with instructions. I'm sure it was all legal. So Windy Scott is dead." The banker shook his head. "He was such a nice person."

"Greed and murder don't take into consideration a man's standing in the community," Splinter said. "Did Scott take the money with him or deposit it here?"

"He took it with him—all five thousand of it. Said he needed the money for his trip."

"How much did Harris steal from the bank?"

"It was close to twenty thousand dollars."

Later on, outside the hotel, Splinter pulled

up a chair and sat down on the porch in the shade. He shoved his hat back on his head and tilted back in the chair. Why all the interest in the Lazy L ranch? What secrets did it hold that would cause murder?

When Ira Crabb came along, Splinter invited him to share his shady spot.

"Thank you," the lawyer said as he sat down. "There's so much going on here, I just can't keep up with it."

"Too bad Santa Nella doesn't have a newspaper," Splinter said. "It would have to put out extras all the time."

"I was in El Cajon for several days with a client, and just got back. I didn't know King Ward had been shot. I hear it happened at the Lazy L."

"Where else? If anything happens, it's connected in some way with the Lazy L."

Crabb nodded. "It certainly seems that way. Too bad about Windy Scott."

"Did you know him?"

"Not too well, but I don't believe anyone here knew him too well. He stayed to himself. I remember one time when he came into town and got drunk at the Glory Be. Told everyone that he had struck it rich. He was also a prospector, you know."

"Never heard that," Splinter said. "So he struck it rich, eh? When was that—before or after he sold his ranch?"

"Before. After he sold it, no one ever saw him again after he rode out of town. Too bad he didn't enjoy the money he got from the sale of his ranch."

"Someone enjoyed it," Splinter said. "Only his gun was found with the body."

Crabb adjusted his glasses on his nose, and then looked at Splinter. "I heard that you are a detective."

"Was. I quit that job. Now I have a job taking care of Peanuts and the Lazy L."

"Doesn't all this trouble interest you? I would think that with your background, you'd be busy trying to solve the crimes."

"It certainly interests me—especially since I happen to be in the middle of it all. But as I said, I gave up detective work, and I'd like to enjoy life."

"Yes, I can see your point. But I also understand that your life has been threatened. Doesn't that fire you up?"

"It doesn't fire me up, but it makes me kinda jumpy. I always try to keep my back against a solid wall."

"Do you really think someone will try to kill you?"

"I sure do—unless I get him first," Splinter replied.

Crabb moved nervously in his chair as he glanced around, realizing his position next to Splinter if anything should happen.

"I believe I shall be moving on," he said, rising. "Nice to have talked with you, McGee."

As he watched Crabb cross the street, Splinter reflected that perhaps he was a fool to stay here, but he now had two strong attachments to the area: Peanuts and Tina.

CHAPTER EIGHT

A week went by with no incidents, and Sheriff Walters sat back in his chair, feet on the desk, a contented expression on his face. Being sheriff of Santa Nella wasn't that bad. Things seemed to be back to normal.

The remains of Windy Scott had been buried with very little fanfare in the little cemetery. King Ward was able to get up a little each day, and Doc Forbes had promised him that he would be able to return to his ranch soon.

Walters was sure that the future would be bright. He had been asked by the commissioners to appoint a deputy, but he told them he was thinking about several men and it would take him time to decide. In reality, he was hoping against hope that Splinter McGee would help him.

He was thinking of these things when Al Harris came into the office.

"What can I do for you, Harris?"

"You might talk McGee into selling his ranch to me."

"I don't believe McGee is selling his ranch to anyone. And it isn't his ranch. It belongs to Peanuts Lane."

"I know that, but the boy will do anything he suggests, so it might as well belong to McGee."

"Just why are you so interested in the Lazy L?"

Harris smiled. "I've always liked it. Wanted to buy it years ago from Scott," he said.

"It ain't worth the price tag McGee and Peanuts put in it.'

"I didn't know they put a price on the Lazy L. How much?"

"Two hundred and fifty thousand."

Harris looked at the sheriff blankly, then slowly shook his head and walked out of the office.

Just then Splinter walked into the office. He jerked his head toward the walk. "What hit Harris?" he asked.

"Your price on the Lazy L."

"I walked past him and he acted like he was in a daze."

"I reckon that price is enough to put anyone into a daze. Where have you been? Haven't see you in a few days."

"Just out lookin'," Splinter replied. "Searched the spot where we found the skeleton, but there's nothing else there. Whoever killed him took that five thousand dollars. No animals would have taken the money."

Walters nodded. "That may have been the motive for killing Windy,"

"As good as any—right now," Splinter said. "I've combed the ranch, trying to figure out why anyone in his right mind would pay good money for the spread. Oh, it's all right, but not worth much. Did you know that Windy Scott had struck it rich just before he sold the ranch?"

Walters shook his head. "What did he strike it rich with?"

"I wish I knew. But usually that expression goes with finding ore."

Walters laughed. "There's no ore around

here that's worth much. Maybe Windy was blowin' off." He added, "Do you suppose someone killed him trying to find out what he struck?"

"That's a possibility."

"Well, at least you're trying. I ain't done too much, I admit. I really don't know where to start. Irish Mulligan always told me what to do, and after four years of that, it's hard to think for myself."

"I know what you mean," Splinter said. "Well, I'm heading back to the ranch. Got some things to do before Peanuts comes home from school."

Splinter reached the ranch in time to fix a little dinner for himself. Then he made a few repairs in the corral. It was already late in the afternoon when he returned to the ranch house and sat down on the porch. He was tired, and it was time for Peanuts to come home from school. He sank back in the chair, looking down the road toward Santa Nella.

He had sent in word with Peanuts to Tina Skelly, inviting her to spend tomorrow, Saturday, at the ranch. He smiled as he thought of her. He hadn't seen her for some time, and he missed her.

He leaned back in the chair and closed his eyes. He wondered what was keeping Peanuts. Perhaps he stayed to talk with Tina after school, which he did now and then. Suddenly, hearing the beat of hoofs on the road, he opened his eyes, expecting to see Peanuts.

Coming toward the ranch house was Peanuts' horse, but no rider!

Splinter leaped off the porch and raced toward the horse. He grabbed the reins and looked at the saddle. There was blood on it!

He gasped as he looked down the road toward town. He pulled the horse down to the stable where he quickly unsaddled it, turning it into the corral. He whistled to Ranger in the corral, and the big horse trotted over to him. He quickly saddled the horse and returned to the house for his rifle. Slipping it into his scabbard, he mounted and headed toward Santa Nella in a gallop.

He was halfway to town when he saw the crumpled body of Peanuts at the side of the road. He drew rein, leaped from his saddle, and fell to his knees beside the boy, who was lying face down in the dirt.

Splinter quickly turned him over. He was breathing. Splinter made a quick examination of the boy. There was a nasty gash along the right side of his head. An arm was badly twisted and probably broken, and his clothes were torn and dirty.

"Shot and dragged!" Splinter muttered as he looked around. He whistled to Ranger. The horse moved in close to them as Splinter got slowly to his feet, holding Peanuts in both arms. He shifted the load slightly as he used his right hand to grasp the saddle horn and pull himself into the saddle.

Holding Peanuts tightly, he lifted the reins and let Ranger have his head as they headed toward town.

"You'll be all right," he assured the unconscious boy. "We'll get you to Doc Forbes right away."

They had traveled nearly a mile when Splinter spotted Peanuts' schoolbooks scattered beside the road. He was sure that the boy had been shot, and then, with his foot caught in the stirrup, he had been dragged to where he found the body.

"Who done it, pardner?" he said as he looked down at the boy in his strong arms. "I'll find 'em—you can bet on that!"

Santa Nella was having a peaceful day as Splinter rode into town carrying Peanuts, but people came running out as he proceeded toward the street where Doc Forbes lived.

Doc was on his front porch, and he hurried out to help carry the boy into the house. Splinter ignored the questions being shot at him by the people who were gathering. He closed the door on them and followed Doc and two men who were carrying Peanuts into a bedroom.

The men placed the boy on the bed. Splinter thanked them and they left as Doc went to work. Splinter leaned against the wall and watched. The door opened and Sheriff Walters came in.

Neither man spoke, but watched Doc Forbes as he opened his black bag and began to work.

"Need hot water from the kitchen," he called out.

"I'll fetch it," Walters said.

"How is he, Doc?"

"He'll pull through. What a beating he took. Right arm broken and badly cut. The gash on the side of his head is bad—but it could be a lot worse."

Walters returned with a bucket of hot water and some towels.

Tina followed him into the room, and Splinter put his arm around her shoulders. No words were spoken, but their eyes talked for them.

The silence was broken when King Ward staggered into the room and looked at the unconscious boy on the bed. He leaned against the door and shook his head.

"Blasted skunk!" he roared. "Hurtin' a little boy."

"You get back to bed," Doc ordered.

"I could kill anyone that'd stoop that low!" Ward growled as Walters took him by the arm and assisted him out.

Splinter, with his arm about Tina, moved over the bed, and they both looked down at Peanuts. Doc, having cleaned the head wound, was working on his arm. Tina turned to Splinter and pressed her head against his chest as Doc set the broken bones. Splinter hugged her tight, his face grim as he watched Doc work.

Walters returned to the room.

When he had finished, Doc said to Tina and Splinter, "It may be some time before he regains consciousness. Let's go into the living room."

There Splinter related what he knew of the event.

"Oh, how horrible!" Tina groaned. "He was in such high spirits when school closed."

"His schoolbooks are scattered along the road," Splinter said.

"I'll get 'em," the sheriff said, shaking his head. "And I thought things were easin' off."

"They won't until we get the person behind all this," Splinter said.

"But how are you going to do that?" Tina asked.

Splinter shook his head. "It ain't going to be easy—unless Peanuts saw who done it. Let's pray that he did."

"He may be hazy for a spell when he wakes up," Doc said. "He took a bad beating and his head especially suffered."

"A great sheriff you are!" a voice snapped. They all turned to see King Ward standing in the doorway, bracing himself against the side of the door. He was weaving slightly, and his face was twisted in pain. "Lettin' a skunk shoot at a little boy!"

"I didn't let him—he just done it!" the sheriff yelled. "Do you think I like it? Get back to bed, Ward!"

Ward leaned forward as though trying to clear his vision, then he pointed a finger at Splinter.

"Now will you get busy and help the law?"

Splinter nodded slowly.

"Stubborn as a pack of mules!" Ward grunted. "Sell me that ranch so you won't be tied down."

"At our price."

"That's plain robbery." Ward turned and went back down the hallway.

Doc sighed and shook his head. "I think I'll send him home," he said. "He gives me more trouble than I care to have."

"How's he comin'?" Splinter asked.

"He could be better, but he won't rest. Why don't you folks go get some supper? Peanuts will probably sleep all night."

"That's a good suggestion," Splinter said. "Let's see what the café has to offer."

When they returned to Doc's house after supper, there was a gathering of townspeople in the yard. Everyone was curious about what had happened and how the boy was progressing.

Splinter and Tina spoke briefly to the peo-

ple, then went into the house, where they
found Ma Anderson assisting Doc Forbes
with Peanuts. King Ward was in the living
room, grumbling because of all the attention
the boy was receiving.

"No one cared if I lived or died," he muttered.

"Tell him, McGee," Doc said, "that there
were people here, but he was unconscious
and didn't know it."

Tina and Splinter nodded, then followed
Doc down the hallway to Peanuts' room. Ma
Anderson was rocking in a chair next to the
bed. She looked up at them and smiled.

"He's resting comfortably," she said softly.

"We appreciate your help," Splinter said.

"Ma's my best nurse," Doc said proudly.
"Always ready to help."

"We'll give you a rest," Splinter offered as
he and Tina moved over to the bed and
looked down at the boy. Doc and Ma left the
room.

"He's so still and white," Tina said softly.

"He's been through a lot." Splinter slipped
an arm about her waist. She looked up at him
and smiled. "All we can do is pray."

"I have—many times since it happened."

She sat in the rocker while Splinter stood beside the bed. He looked at Peanuts, shook his head, and turned to Tina.

"If you have something to do, I'll stay here," he offered. "I plan to stay here until he wakes up."

"What about the ranch?"

"Everything's fine there until tomorrow. I think he'll wake up by morning."

Tina sighed. "I certainly hope so. I wonder if he had a chance to see who shot him?"

"I hope so, but I'm afraid he didn't."

"But why shoot Peanuts?"

"To force my hand, I think. Someone wants me out of the way, and they figured if Peanuts was killed, I'll pull out—but they've got another think comin'."

"Have you any idea who it might be?"

Splinter shook his head. "I have several suspects, but many times it's just the one you don't figure on that's the guilty party. It could be someone who hasn't made a move to purchase the ranch, who's sitting back and throwing the blame on others."

"What is so valuable at the Lazy L?"

"I wish I knew, darlin'. It can't be just that spring. There's got to be something of greater value than that to cause someone to commit murder—in fact, three murders and attempts at King Ward and Peanuts."

"It frightens me," Tina said. "I'm afraid something may happen to you."

They turned and looked at Peanuts. He moved a little under the covers. But that was all. They hoped to see his eyes open. But they didn't.

"I think you should go home," Splinter said. "I'll stay here with Peanuts all night."

Tina rose from the chair, and Splinter took her in his arms and gently kissed her.

"Are you sure you'll be all right?" she asked.

"I'll be fine. Let me walk you home."

Ma Anderson took over the bedside vigil while Splinter walked Tina back home. It was nice out, and the moon was bright, but they were not in the mood for much conversation.

"I'll return the first thing in the morning," Tina said as they reached the Anderson home.

"What about school?"

"Tomorrow's Saturday. I'll stay with Peanuts while you return to the ranch and take care of whatever must be done."

"Peanuts and I certainly appreciate that, darlin'."

"Both of you are pretty special to me," she said softly as he took her in his arms and they embraced.

Splinter dozed off now and then during the night, but there was no change in Peanuts when the room was brightened by sunlight. Doc Forbes was in early to check on him, then he had Splinter join him in the kitchen for a little breakfast.

"He seems to be holding his own," Doc said. "He suffered a lot more than we can see."

"Do you think something inside him might be broken?"

Doc shook his head. "I doubt that, but his whole insides took a terrible shaking when he was dragged. May have shook something loose. We'll just have to wait and see."

"Always wait and see," a voice in the doorway grunted, and they turned to see King Ward. "That's a good solid phrase for doctors to use. Means they don't know."

"Well, we waited for *you,* and now look at you," Doc said. "How is my patient today?"

"Ready to go home," the old rancher snorted as he grasped the door for support.

"Yeah, I'm ready to go home, but how's the kid?"

"About the same," Splinter said. "You've had a long time to think. Have you come to any conclusion why anyone would want to kill you?"

The old man's eyes narrowed and he cursed under his breath, but he shook his head slowly.

"Ain't got the slightest idea," he replied.

"If that bullet had killed you, who would take over your spread?"

"The sheriff asked me that yesterday."

"It's a good question. We never know when our earthly envelope is going to be slit. We ought to be ready."

Ward nodded slowly. "Rogg thinks he's in line to get my ranch, but he's wrong. I have other plans for it."

"Do you have any relatives?"

"That's my business!" Ward snapped. He turned to Doc. "Send word out to the ranch to bring in the buggy and pick me up. I'm fed up with this place."

"I think you're ready to go home. I'll send word out to the Box W."

As Doc left the room Ward limped over and sat down beside Splinter.

"We don't see eye to eye on many things, McGee, but I like your guts. I've had nothing but weaklings around me for so long that I expect everyone to jump when I bark. I've been laid up here for a spell, and it gave me plenty of time to think. Funny how you don't think a lot of the time 'cause you're so darn busy. Well, I've had a lot of time, and I did a heap of thinking. I reckon I've tried to run many people's lives, and I've been successful in a lot of cases. You're the first one that I didn't run, and darn it, I admire you more than those I bossed around. I think most people are afraid of me."

"I appreciate the compliment," Splinter said. "Now level with me—what makes the Lazy L so valuable?"

"Darned if I know," Ward said. "I wanted that spring, but that's all there is on that land. Years ago, I needed that water because my springs had dried up. But Windy Scott refused to sell to me. Some men from back East visited here and made Scott an offer. But he turned them down. Then Al Harris, before he went to prison, wanted to buy the ranch." He shrugged his shoulders. "I don't know why. Harris is a gambler, not a cattle-man. Now, I understand, he wants it again.

But where would he get enough money to buy that land?"

"It's already caused three murders and two attempts. There's got to be more than just the spring water. Those men from the East, have they ever been back?"

Ward shook his head. He shoved his chair back and rose slowly to his feet. "Got to get packed to go home."

Splinter got to his feet as Ward walked unsteadily out of the kitchen. He knew little more now than before his talk with the king of Santa Nella.

Tina Skelly and Ma Anderson were in the living room when Splinter went in there.

"No change in Peanuts," Tina said. "We just looked in on him."

"Doc said it will take time," Splinter said as he ran a hand over his whiskers. He grinned. "Excuse me, ladies, but I reckon I need a shave."

"Take your time at the ranch. We'll manage here just fine, and Ma wants you to join us at her house for supper this evening."

"That sounds great! There's not a lot to do at the ranch, but there is with my face."

Before leaving he looked in on Peanuts. Then he walked outside with Tina while Ma went in with the boy. They stopped on the front porch. Ranger was still tied to the hitch post in front of the house.

"If anything happens, let me know right away," Splinter said.

CHAPTER NINE

WITH his chores completed, Splinter sat on the top rail of the corral fence and slowly surveyed the Lazy L ranch house and surrounding area. As he sat there, Ranger came up behind him and nudged him. He turned and patted the horse on the neck.

Splinter, his eyes nearly closed, studied the ranch house. He had a feeling that his wandering days were about to end, and that he would be living here for a long time. As he looked at the house, he could picture another bedroom added on to it.

"Shucks!" he grunted. "Tina wouldn't want

to settle down with a homely hombre like me."

But his heart told him differently. Since they were both guardians of Peanuts, what could be better than if they married and lived together on the ranch?

A movement near the barn caught his eye. Two calves were standing there. Thinking they might want some water, Splinter slid off the corral fence and started toward them, but they whirled and moved to between the stable and shed, finally going off into the brush. He stopped at the corner and shook his head.

"All right," he said. "I'll drift you around to the waterin' trough."

He sighed and walked down past the shed and around to the rear, where he looked for the two calves, but they were moving farther away.

He had never really been around the shed, only to the front, so he decided to walk around and see what was there. Weeds were growing up close to the building. He walked a few feet, stopped, looked at the ground closely, and kicked the dirt with the toe of his boot. He grunted, knelt down, and fingered the dirt.

"Fill," he said. "Now, why is there fill dirt out here?"

He straightened up and walked around a large area behind the shed. It was all fill dirt, possible a couple of feet deep.

"Just another queer thing," he mumbled. "Maybe Peanuts can tell me where it came from."

He walked around the shed and stopped by its only door. He opened the door and peered inside. There were enough cracks in the walls to give him fairly good light. The place was empty. The old wood floor was clean. There was nothing on the walls. He scratched his head, but something urged him to enter. He moved around the small room. At the far end he paused. There was a hole of about the size of a silver dollar in the floor.

Splinter knelt down and put a finger into the hole. He looked at it closely. It hadn't been a knot in the wood but had been cut there. He again put his finger down into the hole, doubled it up, and pulled up. A section of the floor started to lift.

"Holy henhocks!" he cried as he lifted the floor and peered down into a hole about three-feet square. He set the section of the floor aside and lit a match, looking down into the hole. There was a wooden ladder fastened to one side of the wall. At the top, and just below the wooden floor was an opening where several lanterns rested.

Quickly Splinter moved back to the door and looked outside. No one was around. He closed the door and, noticing a lock and hasp, he fastened it shut, so that no one could walk in on him.

Then he slid over the edge of the floor and down into the hole, his boots resting on a rung of the ladder. He lit a lantern and slowly climbed down into the hole. As he reached bottom, he glanced back to the top. He figured he was a good twenty feet below the surface of the ground.

He looked around. There was a tunnel going off toward the ranch house, and he followed it. The tunnel was about thirty feet long, cut out of rock and dirt and shored up with planks. Henry Lane had been a good engineer. At the end of the tunnel he found several large buckets, two picks, and two shovels.

"The Lazy L. is worth a million!" he said. "No wonder they wanted the ranch. There's gold here."

He set the lantern down and picked up a pick and chopped away at the rock. A small piece fell at his feet and he picked it up and held it close to the lantern. It glistened! He shoved it into his pocket, picked up the lantern, and made his way out of the tunnel.

Splinter replaced the flooring, then opened the shed door and walked outside, his eyes alert to everything. But things were peaceful. He walked up to the ranch house and went inside.

Sitting at the table in the kitchen area, he took out the nugget and looked at it. Slowly he tossed it up and down in his right hand, a broad smile on his face. One of the big mysteries of the Lazy L had been solved—why people wanted the ranch. He pocketed the nugget, got to his feet, and walked over near the bunks where there were several books on a small table.

He chuckled as he picked up one of the books. It was on mining. He had remembered seeing it there. He sat down on the bunk and fingered through the pages. Lane had made notes in the margins throughout the book. Near the end of it, Splinter came across a fancy lettered paper that had been shoved in between two pages. It was a certificate of graduation from the Cincinnati School of Mines.

"Well," he said, "a whole lot is explained now."

Splinter folded the paper and shoved it into his shirt pocket, closed the book and put it back on the table. Then he walked out of the house and headed for the stable.

After saddling Ranger, he led the horse back up to the house. He went inside and came out carrying Peanuts' new clothes. He swung into the saddle and headed for Santa Nella.

Tina Skelly and Doc Forbes were sitting on the front porch of the doctor's house when Splinter rode up. They watched as he dismounted and came up to the porch, carrying Peanuts' clothes.

"Why did you bring Peanuts' clothes here?" Tina asked.

"I thought that when he woke up and saw 'em, it might encourage him to get well faster. How is he?"

"No change," Doc replied. "Ma is in there with him."

Ma was sitting beside the bed, and she

looked up at them. Splinter crossed over and hung the clothes on a hook on the wall. The boy was unconscious, his head wrapped in bandages.

"All we can do is pray—and hope," Tina said softly.

"Is there any change at all, Doc?" Splinter asked.

"His pulse is stronger, but that's all. He went through a terrible ordeal, and it may take weeks for him to recover."

"That long, huh?" Splinter turned to Tina. "Why don't you and Ma take off for a while? I'll stay here."

Splinter had been sitting beside the boy's bed for nearly an hour when Doc Forbes came into the room. He glanced at Peanuts, then stopped in front of Splinter, who was in the rocking chair.

"The sheriff is here and wants to see you."

Joe Walters was standing near the front door, his hat tilted back on his head.

"How's Peanuts?" he asked.

"No change," Splinter replied.

"I hate to tell you this, McGee, but there's word goin' around Santa Nella that maybe you shot the boy."

Splinter's face hardened. He stared at the officer. "Who started that lie?"

"I ain't sure, Splinter, but I think it was Ira Crabb."

"Why would he lie like that?"

"Seems the word is that if the boy should die, you'd get the Lazy L ranch."

"A worthless piece of land," Splinter snapped. "I don't want it—I want Peanuts alive and well!"

The sheriff nodded. "I know you do, Splinter. Just thought I'd let you know what's goin' on."

"Much obliged."

The sheriff hurried out of the house, leaving Splinter standing as though he was in a trance. A sound caused him to turn, and he saw Doc Forbes.

"I heard it. It's a vicious lie!"

"Thanks, Doc. Watch Peanuts. I've got some things to straighten out—fast!"

Splinter was furious. He rushed down Main Street to Ira Crabb's office. It was locked. He crossed to the general store and peered inside, but the attorney was not there. Nor was he at the café. He entered the Glory Be Saloon. Ira Crabb was standing at the bar

with Bat Rogg, Tad Wilson, and Buzz
Crocker of the Box W.

Splinter stopped just inside the swinging
doors, his hands hanging loosely at his sides
as he looked straight at Crabb. The lawyer
slowly turned from the bar and saw Splinter.
He was about to speak to Rogg, who was
next to him, but the sight of the tall cowboy changed his mind. Rogg looked at
Crabb, then over his shoulder toward the
doors.

"Nice bunch of sidewinders!" Splinter
snapped as he started forward, his right hand
swinging freely above his gun. "Crabb, your
loop's draggin'. You better pull it in fast, or
you'll never pull it again."

Crabb glanced at his three companions,
but they were already easing away from him.
None of them wanted any trouble with
Splinter McGee—at least not right now.

"What do you mean?" Crabb said.

"That lie you started about me shooting my
partner!"

Crabb tried to smile, but the effort failed.
He swallowed hard, his Adam's apple bob-
bing up and down. He slowly adjusted his
glasses, his hand shaking.

"I'm sure it was all a mistake," he said slowly.

"It sure was—one of the biggest mistakes you ever made. Lucky for you I'm a patient man, Crabb. All the way here I thought I'd kill you."

Crabb gasped as he stepped backward against the bar, seeking support for his shaking knees.

"Don't you think you're a little strong?" Rogg asked.

"This is none of your business!" Splinter roared. "When I want your advice, I'll ask a rattlesnake."

Rogg reached for his gun, but before his hand was halfway to it, Splinter had his own gun out and was covering the men at the bar.

"That was fast!" Crocker gasped.

"I told you so," Wilson said. "I know how fast he is."

"Crabb," Splinter said, "you and me are going to visit a few people, and you're going to tell them that you're a liar!"

Crab looked at the three men with him, but they offered him no support. He stumbled out of the saloon with Splinter behind him. As they reached the walk, Splinter holstered his gun. He grabbed the attorney by the arm and led him across the road and into the café, which was now filling with people. He held up his hand for silence.

"Folks, Ira Crabb has a few words for you."

Crabb cleared his throat, and with great difficulty he told the people that he had said that perhaps Splinter McGee had shot young Lane in order to obtain the Lazy L ranch, but he was now sure that he had been wrong.

From the café they went to the general store. There were many people there, and they were amused by Crabb's apology, because most of the people in Santa Nella did not like him.

Splinter saw to it that nearly everyone in town had heard Ira Crabb before he took the attorney to his office.

"Let that be a lesson to you to tell the truth," Splinter said as they stopped by the door. "You know that ranch ain't worth much, so why would you tell such a lie?"

Crabb merely shook his head.

"Don't ever say anything like that again. Next time I won't be so easy."

Splinter found a nice supper awaiting him at the Forbes' house. The table was set for three—Splinter, Tina, and Doc.

They enjoyed the meal, and little was spoken. Ma sat beside Peanuts to watch over him. After the meal, Tina and Splinter checked on Peanuts, then went out on the front porch.

Splinter asked Tina, "Why would Ira Crabb try to turn everyone in town against me?"

"I haven't the slightest idea, but from what I've heard, you taught him a lesson."

"There has to be some reason for his doing what he did." He reached into his pocket and brought out the gold nugget. "I believe this is the answer to many questions about the Lazy L."

"Is it gold?"

"Yeah—there's a bushel of it. I found it today, and it answers the question why Lane didn't care to herd cattle. He was mining gold and shipping it out to St. Louis, a little at a time."

"How did he find it?"

"I believe Windy Scott found it. I don't know why he sold the ranch for only five thousand to Lane, but he did. Let's keep this our secret for now, darlin'."

"Oh, yes," she said quickly.

"It's led to bloodshed, and may lead to more

if we can't find out who is behind all the trouble." He paused as a figure appeared out of the darkness, coming up the walk. It was Sheriff Walters.

"Hope I'm not interrupting anything."

"Not at all," Tina said. "I'll go in and check on Peanuts."

"What brings you here?" Splinter asked.

"Just checking on the boy." Walters leaned against the porch pole and tugged at his mustache.

"Peanuts is doing as well as Doc expects. He says it'll take some time."

"Things are quiet in town tonight."

"Did you ever have an assayer around here?"

"No. Anyone who needs an assayer goes to El Cajon. There's a good one over there. Al Harris tried his hand at it years ago. But he had no business, so he had to go back to dealin' cards."

"Maybe I'll talk with Harris," Splinter said.

The Glory Be wasn't busy when Splinter McGee and the sheriff walked into the large room. Al Harris was dealing at one of the card games. He glanced up at the two men, looking for new players, but he realized that neither man would oblige him.

Splinter and the sheriff went to the bar and had a drink as they watched the card games from a distance. Harris's table broke up as the house cleaned out the three men trying to beat him. Splinter moved over to the table and sat down, facing Harris, who was fingering the playing cards on the table.

"No game," Splinter said. "Just a little talk."

"Why should I talk with you?"

Splinter shrugged his shoulders. "You don't have to—unless you want to. I hear you were once interested in assaying."

Harris's eyes narrowed. "That was many years ago."

"Nothing much around here to assay, huh?"

Harris shook his head.

"Did you ever know of any mining in this area?"

"Never was any."

"I heard someone mention that Windy Scott once said that he'd struck it rich," Splinter said.

"Windy said a lot of things. That's how he got his name."

"What makes the Lazy L so valuable?"

"Water," the gambler replied.

Splinter shook his head. "Water's only that precious in hell!"

"I can't see where you and that boy will benefit from keeping that ranch."

"Why do you want it?"

"I've always liked that ranch. I think it would make a fine cattle ranch with all that water."

"You're not a cattleman," Splinter said. "I doubt if you know the first thing about running cattle."

"I can hire good help."

Splinter rose and walked outside with the sheriff. Harris, a smile on his lips, picked up the cards and started to stack them.

"Well?" the sheriff asked Splinter.

"That's about it—that water. It's a good excuse, but it's not the answer. See you in the morning, sheriff."

Splinter hurried down the street to Doc's house. As he came up on the porch, Tina came out the front door and flew into his arms. She was sobbing.

"He's regained consciousness," she said, choking as she spoke.

"That's great!"

"He's conscious, but he doesn't know any of us."

Splinter, his mouth sagging, shook his head. "Did I hear you right, darlin'?"

"Oh, it's awful! Doc is there with him, but he doesn't know any of us."

Splinter took Tina by the arm and then went in to see Peanuts. He was propped up on his pillows, and he looked blankly at them.

"How are you feeling, pard?" Splinter asked.

"Pard—is that my name?"

"No, your name's Jim Lane. We call you Peanuts, but you and I are pardners in the Lazy L ranch."

"Lazy L ranch?" The boy shook his head. "I don't know any Lazy L ranch. I don't know what you're talkin' about, mister."

Splinter looked at Doc, who was sitting on the edge of the bed. Doc shrugged his shoulders.

"It sometimes happens this way," he said as he got slowly to his feet. "Remember, he took a terrific blow to the head."

"Will he stay this way?"

"I really don't know, McGee. Many times it lasts for a short spell, then something shakes their mind and they come back."

"What's that something?" Splinter demanded.

"I can't explain. It has to be like a shock to the mind."

Splinter sat down on the edge of the bed. Peanuts' eyes were bright, but he had a pained expression, as though he was attempting to grasp things. His face was pale in the flickering light of the lamp beside the bed.

Splinter took a deep breath as he looked at Peanuts. "Still thinking of running away?" he asked slowly.

"Runnin' away from what?" the boy asked.

"After your father was killed, you wanted to run away before they sent you to an orphanage."

"Father killed?" Peanuts looked at Tina and Doc, both of them nodding their heads. "I don't know any father. I don't know anyone. I don't even know who I am."

"You're Peanuts—my pardner," Splinter said softly.

Peanuts slowly shook his head. "I'm tired," he said as he closed his eyes.

Splinter looked at Doc, who motioned with his head for them to leave the room. Splinter straightened out Peanuts' blankets, then got to his feet and walked to the doorway. He turned and looked back toward the boy in the bed as Doc lowered the lamp. Then they all left the room and gathered in the living room.

"This is terrible!" Splinter groaned.

"He'll come out of it," Tina said. She put an arm around his waist. "You wait and see."

"But how long do we have to wait?"

"I wish I could tell you, McGee," Doc said.

Just then there was a loud knock at the front door, and Doc opened it. Tad Wilson of the Box W was standing there.

"The Lazy L ranch house is on fire! King Ward saw flames from over that way. He sent me in to get you. Want me to ride with you?"

"No. I'll go out and look."

"I'll stay here," Tina said. "I hope they're wrong."

King Ward was right. Splinter realized it was the Lazy L ranch house as he swung Ranger down a sloping hill toward the house. The building was razed to the ground, with its burning timbers illuminating the barn and shed and the trees, which had escaped the flames.

Splinter dismounted by the corral, and

then walked slowly toward the smoldering heap.

"It's mighty hard to believe—everything gone up in smoke!" he said. "All my worldly goods—extra overalls and two clean shirts."

He chuckled suddenly. "I'm glad I took Peanuts' new clothes with me to town."

When he had ridden into Santa Nella, Splinter had thought of how the ranch house could be enlarged, especially if he and Tina were to get married. Now the ranch house was gone.

"Doggone it all!" he cried. "Once Peanuts is back to normal, we'll have to plan a new ranch house!"

CHAPTER TEN

THE people of Santa Nella were furious when they learned about the burning of the Lazy L ranch house while Peanuts lay wounded and ill.

After visiting the sheriff and Peanuts, Splinter secured a room for himself at the hotel.

"No one's safe anywhere these days," Ma Anderson said at the counter in the general store. "And our sheriff ain't doin' a thing."

"Now, Ma, Joe's doin' what he can," Andy Anderson said. "He needs help. He just cain't be everywhere."

"Why don't the commissioners get help for him?"

"They was hopin' Splinter McGee would help him, but Splinter's got enough to take care of."

"Can't see why the two of 'em can't work together on it."

Andy finished sacking some groceries for a woman.

"I believe your wife is right," she said. "Perhaps if everyone in town got together, they might persuade McGee into assisting our sheriff."

"We'll see what we can do," Andy said as the woman walked out of the store. He looked at Ma. "Thanks a heap. That's what causes trouble in a little town like this."

"I was merely suggestin'," Ma snapped. "I'm going down to see how Peanuts is feeling. Splinter's sleeping at the hotel, and Tina's at school, so maybe Doc can use my help."

"I'm sure he can." Andy watched his wife walk out of the store, passing the sheriff, who was coming in.

"Ma going to Doc's?" Joe Walters asked.

"Yeah. What's new around town?"

"Nothing burned in the last few hours. I

rode out to look at the Lazy L. Man, she's still smolderin'. Burned plumb to the ground."

"Who would want to do that?"

The sheriff shook his head. "Wish I knew, Andy. There's just too many things poppin'—and I'm not doin' a thing to apprehend the ones behind it. Wonder why the commissioners tolerate me as sheriff."

"You're a good man," Andy said.

"Good for what?" Walters snapped as he tugged at his mustache. "All I do is come in after something's been done."

The postmaster stepped into the doorway. "Anyone see Splinter McGee?" he asked.

"He's asleep in the hotel," Andy said.

"A letter was dropped in the slot just a while ago. Thought it might be important."

"I'll take it to him," the sheriff said.

Splinter McGee had been tired when he walked into his hotel room that morning. He threw himself atop the bed and that was all he knew until the sheriff knocked on his door and called out: "Sorry to wake you up, Splinter, but a letter came for you at the post office. I thought it might be important."

Inside, he handed over the letter. Splinter's eyes narrowed as he read the message.

"What's it all about?" Walters asked.

"Listen to this: 'There's nothing left of the Lazy L ranch now, so get out of here pronto or you'll die! Let the kid go to an orphanage. This is the last warning!'"

Walters tugged at his mustache nervously. "What kind of a madman would write that?"

"One that thinks he's got me on the run."

"Any idea who it could be?"

Splinter examined the paper and envelope carefully, then shook his head. "It could be anyone."

"I'm sure everything that's happened here is tied together."

"And it all has to do with the Lazy L ranch."

"That's right. If we knew what the main attraction at the ranch was, we might fight it better."

"I doubt if it would help. I've got to see Peanuts."

As they went down the stairs to the lobby, King Ward, assisted by Bat Rogg, was coming into the hotel.

"They said you was here, McGee," he said hoarsely.

"What are you doing in town? You need to rest."

"I'm doing what I want to—and no doctor's

going to order me around. I was right about the fire, eh?"

"Burned to the ground," Splinter replied as he studied the old man. "Did you come in to gloat about it?"

Ward shook his head. "Nope," he replied sharply. "Maybe now you'll sell the ranch at a reasonable price."

"The price is the same."

"Sure stubborn, ain't he?" Ward said to the sheriff.

"I think both of you are stubborn. What would you do if he sold out?"

Ward rubbed his nose thoughtfully. "Plow what remains under and divert that spring so's it'd reach my land."

"Is that all you're after?" Splinter asked.

"What else is there? That place ain't worth two bits except for that water."

Splinter nodded as his hand dug down into his overall pocket and felt the gold nugget. "You've got my answer, Ward. Now I'm on my way over to see Peanuts."

"I heard about him too." The old rancher shook his head sadly. "Too bad. Thought maybe he could tell who shot him."

"I was hoping for that." Splinter strode past Rogg and out of the hotel.

"That kid means everything to him, doesn't he?" Ward said.

"He sure does," the sheriff replied. "Even to risking his life to help him."

"His life, eh? How's that?"

"I just brought him a letter that warned him to get out of here or be killed. That's the second warning—and he's still here."

"I don't call that very smart," Rogg said. "What chance has he against someone he doesn't know?"

"I have a feeling that Splinter McGee knows something," the sheriff said. "And if he's right, I sure pity that person."

Peanuts was sitting up in his bed, his head heavily bandaged and his arm in a sling. He looked up at Splinter as he walked into the room.

"How are you feeling, pardner?"

"I reckon I feel all right. Doc told me what happened to me. I can't remember a thing."

"You will," Splinter said in a positive voice. He went over to the wall where Peanuts' new clothes were hanging on a nail. He took them down and placed them on the bed beside the boy.

"Remember these new clothes?"

Peanuts slowly shook his head. "Should I know 'em?"

"They're yours. You and Tina bought 'em just a week ago."

"Is she that pretty lady that is here so much?"

Splinter nodded. "She's your school-teacher."

"School? What's that?"

Splinter explained about school, but the boy looked blank. Finally Doc came into the room. He had Splinter hang up the clothes.

"Tina and Ma are in the living room with a pipin' hot meal for us," he said. "I'll check Peanuts, then I'll be there."

Splinter stopped in the doorway and looked back as Doc bent over the youngster. Suddenly something snapped in his mind, and he hurried out of the house, telling the two women that he'd be back in a minute.

Splinter was gone only a few minutes. Smiling, he held up a small white bag as he hurried across the room and down the hallway. Doc was just coming out of the room. He stopped, turned, and went back in, following Splinter who went up to the bed and handed the white sack to Peanuts.

"What's this?" the boy asked as he slowly opened the bag and looked inside. "What are those things?"

The smile faded from Splinter's face as he looked from the boy to Doc. Peanuts turned the bag upside down on the bed, spilling out peanuts.

"I thought you might like some peanuts," Splinter said.

"Peanuts? That's what everyone calls me."

Splinter nodded. "You've always loved peanuts. I thought you'd like some now."

"I don't know anything about peanuts."

Doc put a hand on Splinter's arm and motioned for them to leave.

"That was a good try," Doc said as they walked into the living room.

"Sit down and have supper," Tina said. "We must have patience."

"My patience is runnin' thin," Splinter grunted as he sat down at the table. Tina put her arms around him and kissed him openly before Doc and Ma. They both smiled.

They were nearly through with supper when they heard a noise in the hallway, and they all looked up to see Peanuts moving slowly toward them.

"Young man, what are you doing out of bed?" Doc snapped.

"Wait, Doc!" Splinter cried.

Peanuts paused at the doorway, holding on to the door with his one good hand. He looked at them, then started toward them. When his toe caught on the edge of the rug, he let out a cry as he went down, crashing into a table near the door. His head struck the table.

Everyone jumped up and ran to help him. Splinter picked him up in his arms as the others crowded in. A thin stream of blood oozed from under the bandage.

"Get him back to bed," Doc ordered.

Doc removed the bandage and checked the boy's head. Then he cleaned the cut. He had just put on a new bandage when Peanuts' eyes fluttered and then he groaned. Everyone moved in closer to the bed. Peanuts opened his eyes and looked around, slowly shaking his head, which hurt him.

"What happened?" he asked.

"Don't you know?" Splinter asked.

"I was headin' for home."

"You remember!" Splinter shouted as he sat down on the edge of the bed.

"Didn't you think I'd remember, pard?"

"That knock on the head," Doc said.

"What knock on the head? And what am I doin' here?" The boy observed his arm in a splint. He felt his head.

"Just take it easy," Splinter cautioned. "We'll tell you what happened, but first, do you remember what happened to you when you started for home?"

Peanuts thought for a minute, shutting his eyes as he tried to remember.

"Yeah, I was on my way there when I saw a man on a horse not too far away. Then I heard the sound of a gun—and that's all I know."

"Who was the man?" Splinter asked.

"He was hard to see 'cause the sun was behind him. No, I couldn't tell you who it was."

"Was he the one that shot you?"

"I think so. He was holdin' something in his hands—maybe a rifle."

"I believe that he needs some rest now," Doc said.

"I'm all right," Peanuts said. For the first time he saw the peanuts spread out on his covers. "Gee, peanuts!" He reached out and took some as he looked up at Splinter. "Thanks, pard. I knew you wouldn't forget."

Splinter's eyes moistened and he turned

away as Tina came over to his side and put her arm around his waist.

"I still insist that Peanuts needs rest," Doc said.

Splinter nodded as he put an arm around Tina's shoulders and they walked out of the room. Ma and Doc smiled at them. Then they helped the boy get settled down for a rest.

"It's sure good that Peanuts is back with us," Splinter said to Tina in the living room.

"I knew that he would return in time. He's a strong boy and will progress rapidly now."

Splinter nodded as he sank down in a rocking chair. His mind was relieved of one problem, but there were still others. That note bothered him. He took it out of his pocket and examined it again.

Ma came into the living room and sat down on the sofa.

After a while, Splinter raised the letter to his nose and sniffed it. "Ma," he said, "do you sell much perfume for men?"

"Some," she replied with a smile. "What are you thinking about?"

"Do you recognize this smell?" He handed the letter to her and she smelled it, thought for a moment, smelled again, then handed it back to Splinter.

"I recognize it," she said. "I would say it is our most popular brand for men."

"I wish it wasn't that popular," Splinter grunted.

"Andy could probably tell you more about it. I only sell it now and then."

Splinter nodded and lapsed into silence. He fingered the letter for a minute, then he shoved it into his hip pocket and began to rock back and forth. Tina and Ma looked at each other and winked. They could tell he was thinking deeply.

Finally Splinter got to his feet and paced back and forth. He stopped in front of the sofa and looked down at the two women.

"You ought to go home now," he said. "It's late and Peanuts is coming along fine. I'll stay a spell longer, then go to the hotel."

Tina sensed something in his tone of voice. She nodded and looked at Ma. They both got up.

Tina kissed Splinter, then she and Ma left the house without another word. After they were gone, Splinter walked through the house until he found Doc in a back room checking a medicine cabinet.

"Doc, are you game to trap a skunk?"

"I reckon I am, if it doesn't make too big a smell."

"I don't know much about the smell, but I have an idea. If it works, Santa Nella and the Lazy L can go back to a peaceful existence."

"I'm all for that." Doc smiled. "What can I do?"

"Let's go into the living room and I'll tell you my plan," Splinter said. "If it works, we'll have peace. If it doesn't, there'll be the devil to pay."

CHAPTER ELEVEN

SHERIFF Joe Walters was mulling through reward notices at his desk. He looked up as Splinter entered his office.

"How are things going?"

"Fine," Splinter replied as he sat down on a corner of the desk. "Are you ready for some fireworks?"

"Fireworks? Fourth of July is nearly a month off, Splinter."

"Not that kind of fireworks. I've got me a plan to trap a skunk, but I'm going to need your help."

"You've got it. What's your idea?"

Splinter leaned forward and explained his

plan in low tones. When Splinter finished, Walters drew out his six-shooter and checked it to see that it was fully loaded.

"I'm ready," he said.

"Let's hope it works," Splinter said as he hurried from the office.

The Glory Be Saloon was booming with business when Splinter entered. He stopped just inside the door and looked around. Al Harris was busy dealing at one of the poker tables, and one of his customers was Ira Crabb. Seated nearby and watching the game was King Ward with a drink in his hand. At the bar was the Box W crew—Bat Rogg, Tad Wilson, Lippy Jones, Buzz Crocker, and a few other men.

"How's the boy comin'?" Ward asked Splinter.

Splinter shrugged his shoulders. "No change," he replied.

"That's terrible. When he comes out of it, what a shock it'll be for him to find out his ranch house was burned."

"It sure will."

Splinter crossed over to the bar and ordered a drink, merely nodding to the Box W crew. He leaned back against the bar, hook-ing his right high heel over the railing as he drank slowly and looked over the room. Both poker games were over, and several of the players got up and cashed in their chips. Among them was Crabb, who seemed to have hit a lucky streak. He pocketed his winnings, and, coming up to the bar next to Splinter, he ordered a drink.

"Lucky tonight, eh?" Splinter said.

"It happens once in a blue moon." The attorney smiled.

Splinter smiled, too, as he finished his drink and unhooked his heel from the railing and placed the glass on the bar.

"I'll buy you a drink," Crabb said.

"No, thanks. Just one before bedtime."

"You've certainly been through a lot in the last few days. Burning the ranch house was a mean trick, and just about the last straw."

"Uh-huh." Splinter nodded as he walked away from the bar. Crabb watched him leave the saloon.

Splinter took his time going to the hotel, stopping and looking in the windows along the walk, continually watching to see if anyone was following him. But no one was. As he reached the hotel, he saw the crew from the Box W saddle up and ride out of town.

The hotel lobby was empty. He went upstairs to his room, where he tested the door. It was locked. He took out his key and carefully opened the door, his right hand resting on the butt of his six-shooter. Nothing happened. He stepped into the room and closed the door, locking it behind him. He lit the lamp on the table next to his bed and sat down.

Splinter leaned back on the bed and waited awhile. Then he blew out the lamp. Just in case anyone was watching, he wanted to make it look as if he had gone to bed. Then he got up and walked over to his open window, which looked out on Main Street. He sat down in a chair and waited.

In a few minutes he saw Doc Forbes come around the corner and hurry toward the Glory Be. Splinter smiled as he left his room, this time going down the rear stairs. He wished he could have been in the Glory Be to hear Doc.

Doc Forbes entered the Glory Be and looked around. He acted as though he was out of breath. Everyone turned and looked at him.

"What's the matter, Doc?" King Ward asked as he leaned forward in his chair.

"Anyone see McGee?" Doc asked hoarsely.

"He left a while ago, saying he was going to bed," said Crabb, who was still at the bar.

"I asked you—what's the matter?" Ward growled.

"Peanuts has regained consciousness," Doc replied, looking at the men. "He wants McGee. He saw who shot him!"

Ward's eyes widened. "So he saw who done it, huh?"

"Apparently he did." Doc turned and left the saloon.

Splinter hurried along the dark alley behind the buildings till he was far enough from the light to cross Main Street unseen. Then he continued behind a row of houses until he came to Doc's house, where he climbed through an open window into the room where Peanuts had been.

Splinter glanced quickly around the room, then he froze against the wall as he heard a sound outside. He was to the right of the open window. He held his breath, waiting.

Suddenly a shotgun barrel was lifted over the windowsill, and it blasted away at the bed. Splinter grabbed the barrel and pulled, but the man at the other end had leverage against the side of the house, and he jerked the shotgun loose from Splinter's fingers.

Splinter leaped through the window as the man started across the backyard. Out of nowhere came another man, tackling the man with the shotgun. By the time Splinter reached them, the man with the shotgun had freed himself and was scrambling to his feet. Splinter dove at him, but the man hit Splinter with the barrel of the shotgun, sending him backward, and he fell over the other figure who was trying to get to his feet.

The man whirled in the darkness and ran off across another backyard.

"Darn it!" a voice grunted.

"Let him go," Splinter said. "I think we'll trap a couple skunks before the evening's over."

Sheriff Walters got slowly to his feet. "I should have had him."

"I should have too, but maybe it's best this way. C'mon!"

The officer followed Splinter as they hurried around behind some homes, ran across Main Street, and came in behind the Glory Be Saloon and other stores and offices. Splinter slowed down and took the sheriff by the arm.

"We got to be careful," he said softly. "There's going to be two this time, and a trapped skunk won't give up."

"I'm ready," the sheriff grunted.

Splinter led the way in behind several low structures and stopped at one building where the rear door was ajar. There was a light in the office, and as they moved in closer, they could hear voices.

"You got the boy, eh? That's great," a voice said.

"Now I want to know why you're trying to double-cross me," another voice said.

The sheriff squeezed Splinter's arm. "That's Harris and Crabb," he whispered.

Splinter nodded as they listened.

"Double-cross you? I never thought of such a thing," Crabb said in a nervous voice. "Put that shotgun down."

"After you tell me what you did with all my money," Harris snapped.

"So you discovered that it wasn't there, eh?"

"You knew it all the time. I burned that place just to get my money—and it was gone! All right, where is it?"

"Easy—easy," Crabb cautioned. "Put that shotgun down. It makes me nervous."

"All right," Harris said. "But where's all my money from the bank?"

"I have it in my safe."

"You had it there all the time, but you got me to do all these things for you? Why?

"I want that ranch," Crabb said.

"Not for its water, I bet. There's got to be more than that to get a rich attorney interested in a small ranch like that."

"That's my business!" Crabb snarled. "You'll get all your money from the bank robbery when you kill McGee."

"What about the girl?"

"She'll sell out when I suggest it—especially after McGee is gone. Now you get McGee, and you'll get your money."

"I'll get McGee," Harris said. "And I'd like the Lazy L too."

There was a moment's silence, then the blast of the shotgun shook the small building. The sheriff grabbed the door and pulled it open.

Al Harris was holding the smoking shotgun. Ira Crabb lay crumpled on the floor behind his desk.

"Hold it, Harris!" the sheriff said, pointing his gun.

Harris whirled, but before he could pull the

trigger the sheriff fired. Harris spun around and dropped the shotgun. Then his knees buckled and he fell in a heap.

"Nice shootin'," Splinter said as he rounded the desk and looked at Crabb. "He won't need any medical help."

Walters knelt beside Harris. The man was still alive, although his breathing was jerky. Becoming aware of the commotion outside, the sheriff went over and opened the door. King Ward was in front of the crowd.

"What's happened?" he yelled.

"I'm not sure," Walters replied. He looked at Splinter, who was standing behind him at the door.

"Well, McGee?" Ward demanded.

"All the trouble in Santa Nella is now past history," Splinter said.

Just then Doc Forbes shoved his way through the crowd, and Splinter pointed to Al Harris, who was groaning and tossing on the floor. "Crabb is dead. Harris shot him."

"Who shot Harris?" Ward asked, trying to get into the office. But the sheriff blocked his way.

"I shot him," Walters replied. "It was either him or us."

While the sheriff held off the crowd at the

door, Splinter returned to where Doc Forbes was examining Harris. Splinter knelt down and watched.

"It's bad," Doc told him. "I doubt if he'll live an hour."

Harris groaned, twisted a little, and slowly opened his eyes, looking at the two men. He blinked several times and licked his lips.

"I heard that," he groaned. He licked his lips again, and tried to look around. "Where's Crabb?"

"He's dead," Splinter said.

"How much...do...you know?" Harris asked.

"Enough. Crabb double-crossed you on the bank money, and also forced you to kill Henry Lane and the sheriff. He probably told you he'd give you the money after each job."

Harris nodded as he closed his eyes. "I might as well confess before men now, and wait for the Good Lord to be merciful. Crabb knew I wanted the Lazy L." He paused and took a deep breath. It was an effort for him to talk. "I—I was weak. I went along with him, not knowing that he wanted that ranch too." He stopped, shaking his head.

"Why did you kill the sheriff?"

"After I got away from you and the boy in

the stable, I almost rode into the sheriff. I thought he saw me, so I waited for him."

"Who shot King Ward?"

Harris took a deep breath. He winced with pain as he licked his lips.

"Crabb," he said. "He—he was trying to shot you, McGee. He was a rotten shot."

"Did you shoot Peanuts?" Splinter asked.

"Yes." Harris writhed in pain. "Isn't there something you can do, Doc?"

Doc shook his head. "You better tell it all, Harris. Time's running out."

The gambler sighed and closed his eyes.

"Again, Harris—what was the attraction at the Lazy L?" Splinter asked.

"I don't know," the dying man replied. "I—I just wanted a small ranch with water. After I came back, I wanted it even more when I heard that King Ward wanted it. I hate his guts. He testified against me in the bank robbery."

"Where did you hide that money?"

"Between the two big trees at the Lazy L. I never dreamed that Lane would build over the spot." He paused and licked his lips as he tried to take a deep breath. But it hurt him more now. "I burned the building. I knew no one was there. I was out there earlier this evening, digging. But the box with the money was gone."

"How did Crabb get that money?"

"I don't know. He said he had it. But I didn't believe him."

"How did he know where the money was hidden?"

"He defended me during my trial." Harris paused, sighed, tried to take another deep breath. "I told him I didn't have any money. But we made a deal on the stolen money." He stopped and licked his lips again as he looked at Splinter. "Did—did I kill the boy?"

Splinter shook his head. "I set a trap and moved him to another room. I reckoned that Doc's words would make the guilty one try to keep Peanuts from telling me who shot him. In fact, he talked with me earlier and said he couldn't tell who it was."

"And I fell for it!" Harris gasped.

"Do you know who killed Windy Scott?"

"I think it was Crabb, but I'm not sure." Harris looked around slowly. "Turn up that lamp. It's running out of oil."

Rising to his feet, Splinter looked down at Al Harris as he slipped into the sleep of death.

"I heard it all," the sheriff said.

Splinter nodded. "It's all over. Harris confessed to his crimes before he died."

"What's all over?" King Ward demanded as he tried to look past the sheriff into the room.

"The problems at the Lazy L." Splinter sighed. "I reckon I better get over and tell Peanuts about it."

"What about us?" Ward said. "We want to know what happened!"

Splinter nodded. In a few words he told the crowd what happened.

"Did you suspect either of 'em?" the sheriff asked.

"Crabb used a certain perfume, and that last warning letter smelled of it."

"Why would a lawyer want the Lazy L?"

"There's a large vein of gold on the ranch."

"Gold?" Ward gasped, grabbing Splinter's arm. "Where is there gold on that land?"

"That's what Windy Scott meant when he said he'd struck it rich," Splinter explained. "I found it, but I thought that you, Ward, wanted the ranch for the gold. Crabb knew about it. I think Henry Lane told him about it. Lane mined it and shipped it to St. Louis each month. That's how he existed without cattle."

"I'll be darned!" the old rancher snorted.

Splinter stepped past the men, and as he started down the street King Ward and the sheriff followed him.

At Doc's home, they found Tina and Ma in the living room with Peanuts propped up on the sofa. As Splinter entered, Tina flew into his arms.

"Thank God you're safe!" she cried as she hugged him.

"It's all over," he said as Ward and the sheriff came into the room. "There'll be no more trouble."

"Gee, that's great!" Peanuts said.

"Splinter straightened everything out," the sheriff said proudly.

"I never thought he'd get around to it," Ward grunted. "But I want to know more about that gold."

Splinter grinned as he slipped an arm about Tina's waist and held her tight.

"I reckon it's been there a long time, Ward," he said. "Windy Scott found it, and when Henry Lane came here, he helped the old-timer mine it. Lane was a mining engineer. He bought the ranch because Scott wanted to get away from here, and five thousand dollars seemed a lot of money to the old prospector. Lane built a shed over the opening to the mine, so no one knew where it was."

"I never knew where it was," Peanuts said. "Do you really mean we've got gold on our ranch?"

"Plenty of it," Splinter replied. "Now all we have to do is rebuild the ranch house."

"And make it bigger," Peanuts said.

"He figures thing out." Ward smiled as he held out his right hand to Splinter. "Thanks a million, McGee."

Splinter shook his hand.

"When's the weddin'?" Peanuts asked.

"Weddin'?" Splinter looked down at Tina, whose face was turning red. "Why, I ain't even asked her yet."

"Well, don't take so long," Ma said as she stepped up and hugged Tina and shook Splinter's hand.

Splinter looked at Tina, and she nodded her head and smiled at him. He took her in his arms and kissed her.

"That's it!" Peanuts yelped. "I done heard that a marryin' man needs a best man. How about me, pard?"